CAST OF CHARACTERS

FAMILY SECRETS

*Five extraordinary siblings. One dangerous past.
Unlimited potential.*

Harrison Parker—He's a genius at cracking computer codes, but can the widowed father of three crack the code on love before it's too late?

Maggie Conrad—The Parkers were in trouble—more than they knew—and Maggie was the key to their survival….

Jake Ingram—He's found all of his genetically engineered siblings except for the one who was left behind—potentially the most dangerous of them all!

When you've finished reading
The Parker Project, be sure to look for
the final two books in the thrilling
FAMILY SECRETS series:
The Insider by Ingrid Weaver (on sale April 2004)
Check Mate by Beverly Barton (on sale May 2004)

About the Author

JOAN ELLIOTT PICKART

was very excited when she was invited to take part in the unique and intriguing FAMILY SECRETS series. "I was assigned *The Parker Project*, and Harrison Parker presented a tremendous challenge to me as a writer. He is a troubled man who was not the best husband he could have been to his deceased wife. He is burdened with guilt while attempting to bond with his three children who view him as a near stranger. But when Harrison hires Maggie Conrad as a nanny, magical things begin to happen as the family prepares for the Christmas holidays. Maggie has personal issues to deal with and is none too pleased that her feelings for Harrison are steadily growing."

She hopes you enjoy her part of the FAMILY SECRETS project as well as all the other books that make up this innovative series.

THE PARKER
PROJECT

JOAN ELLIOTT
PICKART

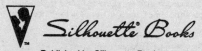
Silhouette Books

Published by Silhouette Books
America's Publisher of Contemporary Romance

Special thanks and acknowledgment are given
to Joan Elliott Pickart for her contribution
to the FAMILY SECRETS series.

 SILHOUETTE BOOKS

ISBN 0-373-61377-6

THE PARKER PROJECT

FAMILY SECRETS

Henry Bloomfield (d.) m. Violet Vaughn 2nd m. Dale Hobson

Susannah Hobson
m.
Travis Dean

Ingram Family

Clayton Ingram m. Carolyn Cook

Zach Ingram
m.
Maisy Dalton

Jake Ingram

Extraordinary Five

Connor Quinn
m.
Alyssa Fielding

Gretchen Wagner m. Kurt Miller

Marcus Evans m. Samantha Barnes

Faith Martin m. Luke Winston

Gideon Faulkner

"Uncle" Oliver Grimble m. "Aunt" Agnes Payne

Evans Family

Russell (Russ) Evans
m.
Lynn Van Allen

Charles Evans
m.
Sarah Alexander

Seth Evans

Drew Evans

Laura Evans

Honey Evans
m.
Maxwell Strong

Holt Evans

——— Birth Family
------ Adoptive Family
m. Married
d. Deceased

For my dear friends
of the First Monday Group
aka Get-a-Hug-Day,
Sharon, Rita and Coty.
Thanks for being there.

One

The winter moon cast a silvery glow over the frost-covered lawns, changing them into magical carpets of sparkling diamonds leading to the Victorian houses that lined the street.

Tall trees with bare branches slept with nature's blessing until it was time to once again produce the multitude of leaves that would provide welcomed shade during the hot, muggy Virginia summer that was months away.

There was a stillness to the night, an aura of peacefulness, as those in the majestic old homes slept beneath puffy eiderdowns and marshmallow-soft blankets.

But in one house a light shone behind the curtains of an upstairs window. The glow was dimmed by a fleeting shadow that disappeared, then reappeared. Back and forth, there, then gone, then back again in a slow, steady rhythm.

Inside the quiet room Harrison Parker paced, a deep frown on his face, one hand hooked over the back of his neck as he attempted and failed to find answers to the multitude of questions beating against his beleaguered mind.

With a sigh he sank onto the old leather chair behind the desk in the office he'd created in one of the spare bedrooms. He glanced at the clock on the desk and shook his head.

One-fifteen in the morning, Harrison thought. He had to go to bed and get some sleep, but dreaded the image of tossing and turning, dozing and waking, then facing the new day just as exhausted as he had been the day before and the one before that.

"Ah, hell," he said, leaning his head back on the top of the chair and staring at the ceiling. "What am I doing wrong? Nothing I try is working. Nothing."

Nine months, he thought. It had been nine long months since his wife, Lisa, had been struck by a drunk driver as she'd been driving home. She'd been killed instantly, they had told him, hadn't suffered. She had simply ceased to exist, was gone. Forever.

Nine months. And for eight of those months, Harrison knew, he'd functioned in a fog of grief and pain, burying himself in his work so he could buffer the loneliness, anger and self-pity. For eight months he'd been vaguely aware of his three children, listening to them but not hearing what they were saying, seeing them but not comprehending what they needed from him, talking to them but not remembering moments later what he had said.

He'd placed his David, Chelsey and Benny in the care of a nanny, then escaped from the tears echoing within the walls of this house that used to ring with the sound of laughter.

The nannies quit, one after another, stating they couldn't control his defiant children who refused to follow directives and were totally out of control. Rather than address the issues, he'd simply hire another victim, who would last a few weeks, then flee.

Then a little over a month ago, Harrison mused on, the nanny informed him, as he handed over her last check, that his youngest son, four-year-old Benny, had thrown a tantrum and broken a dozen knick-knacks that had belonged to his mother. Even worse, Benny often went days at a time without speaking, a horrifying fact that Harrison hadn't even noticed.

"Father of the Year, that's me," Harrison said aloud, then dragged his hands down his beard-roughened face.

He'd dragged himself out of his mental and emotional pit of despair, quit his job as the top computer expert at the prestigious corporation where he'd climbed steadily to the top of the ladder, and set about opening his own computer consulting business at home.

He would take care of his brokenhearted children. *He* would repair the damage he'd done to them by ignoring their grief as he'd wallowed in his own. *He* would turn them back into the vibrant, happy kids they had been, and they'd get on with their lives, move forward. Without Lisa. Somehow.

"Yeah, right," Harrison said, a weary edge to his voice. "And what a helluva fine job you've done in the past month, Parker. Progress…zip, *nada,* none."

Ten-year-old David was sullen and rebellious and informed his father at least once a day that he hated him. Seven-year-old Chelsey was sucking her thumb, which she hadn't done since she was in diapers. And Benny? If he said six words from the time he got up until he went to bed at night it was a red-letter day.

His family couldn't go on like this, Harrison thought, pushing himself to his feet. He'd lost his wife, and he was slowly but surely losing his kids despite all his efforts to make them feel safe and loved and…

"Sleep," he said, turning off the lamp on the desk. "I need sleep. Tomorrow—well, today—is Saturday and we'll do something fun together. Yeah. That's the ticket. Fun. I'm an intelligent, thirty-three-year-old man, for cripe sake. I can do this. I just have to figure out how and I will. Damn it, I will."

The next morning Harrison placed plates of pancakes in front of the children where they sat in total silence at the big oak table in the large kitchen.

"Hey, guys, take a gander at those," he said, forcing a brightness to his voice. "Pretty jazzy, huh?"

"What is it?" David said, leaning forward and peering at his plate.

"It's one of Santa's reindeer," Harrison said. "The antlers stuck to the griddle but that's what it is—a reindeer. And, Chelsey, you have a Christmas bear, except I sort of burned his hat but…Benny, look at your pancake, buddy. It's a Christmas tree.

See? December snuck in the door when we weren't looking, troops, and we've got lots of great stuff to do together during the next weeks to get ready for the big day. Santa Claus is coming to town.''

"Whoopee," David muttered, then picked up his fork and poked the pancake. "Dad, this is as hard as a hockey puck. It isn't a reindeer, it's a rock."

"Oh," Harrison said, frowning. "Well, wait. The syrup will soften them up. That's what syrup does...I think. Does anyone know where the syrup lives in this place?"

Chelsey pulled her thumb from her mouth. "It's next to the jelly in the cupboard by the sink, Daddy."

"Right," Harrison said, opening the cupboard door and staring at the glaring empty space. "We don't have any syrup. I'll put it on the shopping list and... So! Who wants some cereal?"

A short time later, Harrison shoved the empty cereal bowls to one side on the table and sank onto a chair with a cup of coffee and the morning newspaper. He tuned out the sound of cartoons on the television in the living room that were being watched at a volume that could probably provide entertainment for two or three neighboring houses in each direction.

"That certainly went well," he said, picking up the reindeer pancake.

He dropped it back onto the plate and his eyes widened as the china dish cracked down the middle.

"The Defense Department could probably use these as a secret weapon," he said, shaking his head.

Sipping the hot coffee, he began to read the newspaper, scanning the headlines for something of interest. When he came to the entertainment section, he spread out the paper and leaned over it.

"Fun. Think fun," he said. "Hey, here we go."

A story hour would be presented by the children's librarian, Maggie Conrad, at two o'clock that afternoon, Harrison read, and children of all ages were invited to attend.

Harrison nodded. This was good. He'd drop off the kids at the library, then go Christmas shopping, really get a jump on purchasing the perfect gifts for his brood. Afterward they would go out for ice cream together and they could tell him all about the story they'd heard. Perfect.

In the meantime he needed to clean the kitchen, do a couple loads of wash, spit-shine the bathrooms, if he could remember where he'd stuck the supplies the last time he'd scrubbed and rubbed.

"Jeez," Harrison said, getting to his feet. "No rest for the wicked."

How had Lisa managed to do it all? he wondered as he began to clear the table. A couple of years ago he'd offered to hire a cleaning lady for her but she'd refused, saying she'd rather tend to her own home. Well, if Lisa could do it so could he.

Lisa, Harrison thought, frowning as he continued his chores. During the months leading up to the accident he'd rarely made it home for dinner. He'd spent a great deal of time in Washington, D.C., working on various projects with the government agencies that had hired his firm, or to be more precise, him.

It was no wonder he'd lost the connection between himself and his children. They were most often asleep by the time he'd arrived home, and he left the house in the morning before they were awake.

Lousy father, he thought, his frown deepening. And lousy husband. He'd centered on his career and left Lisa on her own to handle everything else. Had she been unhappy and he'd missed the clues that she was less than satisfied with the direction their marriage was taking? How long had it been since they'd made love, shared a meal, been out on a date, per se, just the two of them, before she was killed? He couldn't even remember.

He could never make it up to Lisa, not now. He'd have to live with the guilt of his neglect of her for the rest of his life. But he *could* repair the damage he'd done to the relationship with his children.

Harrison spent the remainder of the morning attempting to complete the mental list of tasks he'd made for himself. His frustration grew steadily as he put too much detergent in the washing machine and huge mounds of wet bubbles poured out onto the laundry room floor, then slithered toward the kitchen.

He knocked over a carton of milk in the refrigerator, which resulted in having to remove everything inside to mop up the mess. He discovered two containers of some strange stuff that was covered in mold on a bottom shelf and pitched them out, containers and all.

When he leaned over the edge of the bathtub to scrub it, he reached up to turn on the water to rinse off the scouring powder and tripped the switch that caused the shower to come on and drench him in cold water.

And through it all, cartoons bellowed from the living room where his kids sat like zoned-out zombies, totally oblivious to what was going on around them.

When he made peanut butter and jelly sandwiches for lunch, Chelsey burst into tears, sobbing out the information that she only liked peanut butter and butter sandwiches, and Mommy knew that, and how come he didn't know that, and she wasn't going to take one bite of that glob with the jelly, not one. Harrison replaced the sandwich with one made to Chelsey's specifications, then sank wearily onto the chair next to David at the table.

"Eat," Harrison said. "We're going to a really cool deal in a little while."

"What is it?" Chelsey said, still sniffling.

"A very special event at the library," Harrison said, forcing as much enthusiasm into his voice as he could produce. "There's a story hour being put on and I'm going to drive you into town so you can enjoy it and then we'll go for ice cream when it's over."

"Story hour?" David said, nearly shrieking. "That's for babies, Dad. I don't want to go to a stupid story hour. What if some of my friends see me in the baby room at the library? No. I'm not going to a lame story hour.''

"You're going, David," Harrison said, narrowing his eyes. "This isn't open for discussion."

"I hate you," David said, jumping to his feet.

"Whatever,' Harrison said, his shoulders slumped. "You're still going to the story hour...and you're going to have fun while you're there. Got that?"

David glared at his father, then spun around and stomped from the room.

"David doesn't really hate you, Daddy," Chelsey said, then paused. "Well, maybe he does. I don't know." She stuck her thumb in her mouth.

"Chelsey," Harrison said, "eat your sandwich. You can have that thumb for dessert, although you're a tad old to be sucking your thumb, don't you think? Benny doesn't suck his thumb."

On that cue, Benny popped his thumb into his mouth. Harrison swallowed an earthy expletive and left the table.

Just before two o'clock Harrison entered the library with a scowling David, a thumb-sucking Chelsey and a silent Benny.

A woman in her sixties happened to be passing the doors at the time, said she was the reference librarian and could she be of assistance? Harrison explained why they were there and the woman said she would be happy to deliver the children to the room where the story hour was being held. Harrison thanked her and beat a hasty retreat.

A little over an hour later a thoroughly discouraged Harrison returned to the library. He'd wandered through a large shopping mall that was decorated to the nines for the holidays and had Christmas carols blaring from unseen speakers. He'd gone from store to store, finally having to admit to himself that he had no idea what would make perfect gifts for his children because he'd lost touch with who his children were.

Lousy father.

Harrison entered the ancient but well-maintained library with the intention of using its computers to do some research for one of the projects he was now privately contracted for while he waited for the kids.

But as he crossed the gleaming wooden floor his attention was caught by the delightful echo of children's laughter. He wandered in the direction of the joyous sound, allowing it to fill him to overflowing, warm him from head to toe as he realized how long it had been since he'd heard his own children's laughter dancing within the walls of their home.

He stepped just inside the room where more than a dozen children were sitting on the carpet and swept his gaze over the enclosure.

It was a child's paradise, he mused, with beanbag chairs and large, cotton-ball-soft pillows on the floor. There was a mural of smiling animals painted on one wall and bright tables and chairs scattered among the multitude of bookshelves.

Harrison eased farther into the room and leaned one shoulder against the back wall, crossing his arms over his chest. He looked toward the front of the room and his gaze fell on the attractive woman who had short, curly blond hair, appeared to be in her late twenties and who obviously had the children enthralled with the story she was telling. She was dressed in baggy slacks and a huge red sweater and had a pair of reindeer antlers on her head.

Pretty lady, Harrison mused. Certainly not the stereotype librarian that the word conjured up in a person's mind. She was prancing back and forth, really giving it her all.

Jeez, David was so captivated by the performance that his mouth had dropped open and his eyes were riveted on— What was her name? Oh, yeah. Maggie. Maggie Conrad. Chelsey wasn't sucking her thumb and Benny had a big grin on his face. They sure didn't look like the sullen, grumpy kids he'd dropped off here.

"Oh, help me, help me," Maggie said, leaning toward her audience. "If we don't find Clarence the bunny in time he'll miss Christmas. I'm Daisy the deer and all my friends here in the woods are calling to Clarence but he isn't hearing us. We must find him in time for Christmas. Please help me. Hurry. Hurry."

To Harrison's amazement all three of his kids, including the silent Benny, began to call for Clarence, causing a smile to break across Harrison's face.

Maggie Conrad had no idea, Harrison thought, that she was casting a magical spell over the Parker children.

"Hush, hush," Maggie/Daisy said. "I think I hear something. Shh. Do you hear something?"

Every little head in the group nodded.

"Oh, oh," Maggie said. "There he is. There's Clarence and just in time. Oh, no, he's turning the wrong way. He's going farther into the woods. We must do something. I know. Let's clap our hands and call his name as loud as we can so he'll hear us. Clarence!"

Benny jumped to his feet, clapping his hands. "Clarence, Clarence. Over here, Clarence. Hurry, bunny, so you don't miss Christmas."

Man, Harrison thought, feeling his throat tighten with emotion. Look at his son. His baby boy who hardly spoke a word at home. And David and Chelsey were clapping and calling to the bunny, too.

"He's here," Maggie shouted, then wrapped her arms around an imaginary something, making the whole thing so real that Harrison would have sworn she was hugging a bunny named Clarence.

"Thank you so much for your help," Maggie said. "And thank you for coming today. I hope you'll visit me again very soon." She bowed, then straightened and blew kisses to the children. "Goodbye for now."

"Goodbye," the children answered, then got to their feet and started toward the door.

Harrison pushed himself off the wall and glanced to the side, seeing the parents who were waiting for their excited, chattering offspring just outside the room.

He redirected his attention to the front of the room and frowned slightly as he realized that his three weren't looking for him. They had moved forward to gather around Maggie Conrad.

"You were such a big help in finding Clarence," Maggie said, smiling at each of them in turn. "Thank you so much. You deserve a hug from all the animals in the woods and especially from Clarence."

Uh-oh, Harrison said, starting toward the front of the room. This could get sticky. All his attempts to hug his children in the past month had resulted in them stiffening and twisting out of his arms. He didn't want what had obviously been a fun outing to end in disaster.

Harrison stopped dead in his tracks as he watched Maggie hug each of his children and saw them fling their arms around her neck when it was their turn. When she released Benny, he grabbed one of her hands with both of his.

"Can you come to our house, Maggie?" Benny said. "We'll be good. Honest. And you could tell us another story."

"That would be cool," David said. "We wouldn't make you eat anything our dad cooked. We could maybe get a pizza delivered or something so you wouldn't croak from what my dad makes. Wanna come?''

"Please?'' Chelsey said. "I won't suck my thumb while you're there. I promise.''

"You're all so sweet,'' Maggie said, then dropped a quick kiss on the top of each of their heads. "Thank you for the invitation, but I'm afraid I have to stay here because working in the library is my job.'' She paused. "Your father doesn't cook too well, I take it? Do you mind if I ask where your mother is?''

"She's an angel in heaven,'' Chelsey said.

"An angel,'' Benny said, nodding. "In heaven.''

"I see,'' Maggie said quietly. "Well, both my mother and father are angels in heaven so I understand that you must miss your mother very much. But don't forget to be thankful that you have your dad.''

David lifted one shoulder in a shrug. Benny frowned. Chelsey stuck her thumb in her mouth. A chill swept through Harrison.

"Hey,'' he said, forcing a smile as he closed the remaining distance between himself, Maggie and the children, "are you the Parker kids who just helped find Clarence the bunny? Yes, sir, I believe that's who you are, all right. I was getting worried that Clarence was going to miss Christmas, that's for sure.''

He shifted his gaze to Maggie and extended his hand. "Hello, I'm Harrison Parker, Ms. Conrad, and these are my children, David, Chelsey and Benny. I have to confess that every word my mouthy kids just said about my cooking is true. I'm a dud.''

He was a gorgeous dud, Maggie thought, unable to tear her gaze from Harrison Parker's blue eyes that seemed to be pinning her in place and making it difficult to breathe.

Her hand floated upward of its own volition, it seemed, and was grasped by Harrison's.

''It's a…it's a pleasure to meet you,'' Maggie said, feeling a strange heat travel from her hand up her arm, then tingle across her breasts. ''You have…'' The most enticing thick blond hair, and rugged good looks, and a blatant masculinity that is absolutely terrifying. ''…adorable children.''

A summer sky, Harrison thought, reluctantly releasing Maggie's hand. Her eyes were as blue as a summer sky. She was fairly tall, maybe five foot six, but her oversize clothes didn't give a hint as to what kind of figure she had. Her features were delicate and those lips… Damn, those were kissable lips. Oh, man, Parker, where was all this coming from? Knock it off.

''Okay, guys, thank Ms. Conrad for the fun time,'' he said. ''We have to get going.'' He looked at Maggie again. ''Or maybe it's Mrs. Conrad?''

''No,'' she said, looking at the children and not at Harrison. ''I'm not married and Maggie will do just fine. I hope you'll come to story hour again.''

''If you came to our house…'' David started.

''David,'' Harrison said, ''Maggie has work to do

here at the library. Come on. We're going for ice cream, remember?''

"It's too cold out for ice cream," David said, frowning. "Ice cream is a dumb idea on a cold day."

"Then have hot chocolate, David," Maggie said, "with marshmallows on top. Yummy. I wouldn't be frowning like that if someone was going to let me have hot chocolate with marshmallows."

"Does Clarence the bunny like hot chocolate?" Benny said.

"Oh my, yes," Maggie said. "I serve it to him whenever he comes to visit me."

"'kay," Benny said. "Then I'll have some hot chocolate." He started hopping toward the door. "I'm Clarence, I'm Clarence, I'm Clarence."

"Are not," Chelsey said. "I am. I can hop better than you, Benny Parker."

"Oh, brother," David said, rolling his eyes as he started after his siblings, "they are such babies."

"Wait for me by the front door," Harrison called to the trio as they left the room. He looked at Maggie again. "You have no idea what you accomplished here today with my children. My wife was killed in an automobile accident nine months ago and it's been rough going ever since.

"They've gone through a string of nannies to the point I've lost track of how many they've sent packing. I'm in charge now and I have to admit that I'm not doing very well with them, either. They're hurt, angry, sad…you name it.''

Maggie nodded.

"To see them so animated, acting so much like they used to while they listened to your story," Harrison went on, "was really something, gave me a morale boost that I needed, believe me."

"Well, I'm glad you brought them to hear about Clarence," Maggie said, then took a step backward as she wrapped her hands around her elbows.

Harrison Parker, she thought, was standing too close to her, was in her space, her comfort zone. He was just so male, and just so big, and just so…there. She wasn't at ease around men like Harrison who exuded such raw and earthy masculine sensuality. Actually, she wasn't that comfortable around adults in general, definitely preferred to deal with children.

"Dad," David said, from the doorway, "are you coming, or what?"

"Yes. Yes, I'm on my way, David," Harrison said. "Thank you again, Maggie. I'll see—we'll see you again, I'm sure. Man, I wish you had a twin sister, or a clone or something, who would love being a nanny to my brood. You'd be perfect in that role. Goodbye for now."

"Goodbye," Maggie said quietly, as Harrison strode to where David was waiting with a less-than-sunny expression on his face.

Such beautiful children, she mused. David and Benny had blond hair like their father, and Chelsey had dark curls that she probably inherited from their mother. Who was an angel in heaven.

A shiver coursed through Maggie as she glanced around the empty, silent room.

But the Parkers were still a family. They had each other to lean on, seek comfort from, laugh and cry, share and care, as they learned to move forward with their lives.

Yes, they had each other.

They weren't alone.

Like she was.

Two

Just after eleven o'clock that night, Harrison shut down the computer, then yawned as he rotated his neck in an attempt to loosen the knotted muscles.

He was exhausted to the bone, he thought, but at least he was headed for bed at a decent time and would hopefully be able to chalk up hours of rejuvenating sleep. The fact that he and the kids had spent a decent day together might just help in his getting a peaceful night's sleep.

It *had* been a good day. They had gone to a café for hot chocolate after leaving the library, and Benny had said he wanted to order a mug of the hot drink for Clarence the bunny. The fact that Benny had that much to say was so great, Harrison thought, he would have bought Clarence a Lexus to drive home in.

To Harrison's amazement David didn't launch into a dissertation of how dumb and babyish Benny was acting, and had even gone so far as to tell his little brother that Clarence only liked one marshmallow on the top of his hot chocolate. Not two, just one.

The waitress had gone along with the whole program, Harrison thought, a smile tugging at the corners of his mouth. She'd returned with the tray of drinks, with an extra one for Clarence.

"It's hot," she said. "Wow, do bunnies know how to blow on hot stuff to cool it off?"

"I'll blow on it for Clarence," Chelsey said.

He'd stifled a hoot of laughter, Harrison recalled, when David volunteered to drink Clarence's chocolate because the bunny had had a big lunch and had said he was too full for a treat.

Harrison got to his feet.

The evening that followed hadn't been spectacular, he thought, as David had done his usual disappearing act into his room, Chelsey resumed the thumb-sucking thing and Benny had nothing further to say.

But, by golly, there had been a few hours in there when they had interacted like a family, laughing, sharing, having a good time.

Thanks to Maggie Conrad.

Harrison stared into space. Maggie was an intriguing woman, as well as an attractive one. When she'd been performing for the children, she'd seemed to almost glow with delight as she took on the persona of the animals in the woods. She was a really dynamite storyteller, no doubt about it.

But when he'd begun to talk to her, she had tensed up, withdrawn somehow, seemed to erect a protective wall around herself. Why? There was nothing intimidating about him, was there? Surely he hadn't done anything to make Maggie feel threatened, yet she'd become edgy, nervous, avoided looking directly at him.

A complicated lady was the lovely weaver of tales, Harrison thought, reaching toward the lamp. And not one to be easily forgotten.

Before he could shut off the light, the telephone on the desk rang, causing him to jerk at the sudden, unexpected noise. He snatched up the receiver, not wanting the shrill sound to wake the kids.

"Parker," he said.

"Tynan," a man said.

"Matt?" Harrison said, smiling. "How are you? I haven't heard from you since..." His smile faded. "Hey, thanks for the flowers you sent when Lisa... I should have called you, or written a note but it was a rough time and... No, there's no excuse for not acknowledging the bouquet. I appreciate your sending it."

"No thanks are necessary," Matt Tynan said. "I wanted to come for the funeral, but it was impossible for me to get away. I'm sorry I wasn't there for you, Parker. How are you doing? And the kids? Man, it's got to be so hard on them to have lost their mother, not that it's any picnic for you to have lost your wife. You hanging in?"

"Yeah," Harrison said, sinking back onto the chair. "One day at a time."

"Whatever works, I guess." Matt paused. "Listen, I heard you quit your job a few weeks ago and started your own company, sort of freelancing out of your house.''

''Now that's the Matt Tynan I recognize,'' Harrison said, chuckling. ''If it happens, you know about it. The kids were wiping out nannies as fast as I could hire them. I decided that they needed me to be here, but I'm not exactly turning them back into little bundles of smiles and sunshine. But like I said, one day at a time.''

''Time is the key word there, I think,'' Matt said. ''That's what it's going to take for all of you to be able to move forward.''

''Yeah, I suppose.''

''Listen, Harrison, I realize I'm calling at a socially unacceptable hour, but this is important. Are you free to talk?''

''Sure.'' Harrison propped his feet on the edge of the desk and crossed them at the ankles. ''What's on your tiny mind, Matt? I've never known you to call to just chat. You want something. Spill it. I'm all ears.''

''Okay,'' Matt said. ''I'm going to tell you a story, my friend, that you'll find hard to believe, but I assure you that every word is true.''

''Does this tale of yours have a bunny in it named Clarence?''

''What?''

''Never mind,'' Harrison said. ''Go ahead.''

''This is top secret, Harrison. All of it. The background I'm going to give you and what I need from you is all highest security. Big time.''

"No problem.''

"I'm going to need your expertise at computer hacking, old chum. If you get caught you're going to be in trouble up to your eyebrows, plus you'll lose the security clearance you have for those government jobs you're taking on to feed the kiddies. You don't have to do what I'm asking unless you really want to. Understood?''

"Yeah,'' Harrison said, chuckling, "and I also understand that you've run an extensive and recent background check on me. Since I only opened my own business here at home a month ago, how is it you know about my government projects and the level of security clearance I have with Uncle Sam? Clearance I was able to keep despite leaving the company where I was working.''

"You're not the only hacker in the world, Parker,'' Matt said, laughing. "You just happen to be one of the very best, plus I know I can trust you. I need that combination in place.''

"Slow down a minute here,'' Harrison said, frowning. "From what you're saying I will be risking an awful lot if I take on this project. You and I have been friends for many years, Matt, but I have to put the welfare of my kids first.

"Starting my own business is shaky enough without possibly losing my clearance rating or getting into some kind of trouble you're hinting at that could result in not having a business or income at all.''

''I hear what you're saying,'' Matt said. ''Put our years of friendship aside for a moment and center on the security you'd have for those kids with the money I'm in a position to pay you for coming on board.''

''Speak,'' Harrison said.

Matt named a figure and Harrison whistled as his eyes widened.

''That's a lot of peanut butter sandwiches, buddy,'' Harrison said. ''It would relieve my stress in the financial arena knowing I had a nest egg like that for the kids.'' He took a deep breath and let it out slowly. ''Okay. I'm in. Let's hear your story, Tynan.''

Almost an hour later, Harrison shook his head and let out a pent-up breath, realizing he'd nearly stopped breathing as he'd listened to what Matt was saying. At some point that Harrison was totally unaware of he'd dropped his feet to the floor, every muscle in his body tensing as he tightened his hold on the telephone receiver.

''Unreal,'' Harrison said finally. ''Unbelievable. Genetically engineered babies who are now adults and… It's like a sci-fi movie, Matt. At least you guys decoded that set of false notes, which would have misled anyone trying to duplicate the experiments. There's a fair chance that no more of those babies could have been produced. But… Man, this is potent, dangerous stuff you're talking about here.''

"No joke," Matt said. "And I don't think you'll have any difficulty understanding why I need you to get into the Medusa files and obtain the data from Code Proteus and Achilles."

"Achilles is Gideon," Harrison said. "The only one of the original group of genetically engineered babies you've been unable to locate now that they're grown up."

"Yes, and we've got to find him as soon as possible," Matt said. "This is going to take a lot of concentrated time on your part, Harrison. Tell me now if you don't feel you can do it because of the situation you're in with your family."

"I'll figure out a solution to that," Harrison said. "There's no way I'm bailing out on this before I even get started. I'll access those files, Matt, and get you what you need. Damn, what an incredible scenario this is. You can count on me."

"I guess I knew that before I even picked up the phone to call you," Matt said. "Thanks, Harrison. Let me give you a couple of numbers where you can reach me 24/7. I take it that I don't have to repeat how much is at stake here?"

"No way. I read you loud and clear. Give me the phone numbers."

A few minutes later Harrison replaced the receiver, aware that his hand was trembling slightly. He replayed in his mind the entire conversation with Matt Tynan, shaking his head in wonder when he finally got to his feet again.

As he started to reach for the switch on the lamp, he stopped and flattened his hands on the top of the desk, frowning into space.

This changed things, he thought. He couldn't come into this office to work on the project for Matt as mentally wiped out as he had been after battling with his kids. He had to have some help with his children so he could still be sharp after they went to bed. But where in the hell was he going to find someone willing to take on his brood? The word was probably out among the nannies of the world to steer clear of the Parker household.

Benny went to preschool for a half-day session, but all the kids were about to be turned loose from school for the long vacation surrounding the holidays.

Harrison snapped off the lamp and started slowly from the room, his shoulders slumped with the bone-deep fatigue that suddenly consumed him once again.

Who he needed to solve his dilemma, he thought with a weary sigh, was magical Maggie Conrad.

Several hours later, Maggie gave up her attempt to sleep and left her bed, which was a tangled mess of sheets and blankets. Shoving her feet into fuzzy slippers and tugging on a faded terry cloth robe she went into the small kitchen of the guest house she rented in the back of a large estate and fixed herself a mug of hot milk.

With a weary sigh she sank onto one of two chairs

at the round table against the wall. Propping her elbows on the table, she nestled the mug in her hands and took a sip of the steaming liquid.

She was so furious at herself she could scream, Maggie thought, frowning. She had tossed and turned for hours because of the haunting image of Harrison Parker that refused to budge from front row center in her mind.

She could see him now so clearly it was as though he was there with her in her minuscule kitchen. He was so tall, his shoulders so broad, his features so rugged. His thick blond hair was badly in need of a trim and those blue eyes of his were capable of stealing the very breath from her body.

"Oh-h-h, this is ridiculous," Maggie said, then took a big swallow of milk.

Why, why, why was this happening to her? Harrison Parker had intimidated her with his blatant, male sexuality, had made her edgy and uncomfortable when he'd stood so close to her in the children's room at the library. She registered a tremendous sense of relief when he'd finally left to take his children out for hot chocolate.

No, she had to be honest with herself. The relief had lasted about ten seconds, then had been replaced by a strange chill as though Harrison had been the source of heat to warm her. She'd felt so incredibly alone after he had gone. Alone and lonely.

Maggie plunked the mug onto the table and pressed her fingertips to her now-throbbing temples.

Ridiculous was too lightweight of a word for all of this, she fumed. Her reaction—no, *overreaction,* to Harrison Parker was crazy, totally insane. She had vowed, and meant it, that she would never again succumb to her own feminine desires that might be brought to the surface of her being from the dark, dusty corner where she'd put them forever.

Once, just once, in her twenty-seven years she'd gathered her courage and trusted a man she truly believed loved her, cared for her as much as she cared for him.

Oh, ha. What a joke that had been. After being together for nearly a year he'd taken a job overseas, said thanks for the memories, toots, and walked out of her life without a backward glance.

Never again. Never again would she venture into the man-and-woman-engaged-in-a-relationship arena. She'd managed, with time, to put her shattered heart back together but envisioned it as being extremely fragile, able to be easily smashed to smithereens once again, which was a risk she would never, ever take.

And even if she'd managed to piece her heart back into reasonable shape with Super Glue to the point where it was strong and steady, she'd *never* go anywhere near a man like Harrison Parker. No. He was just too…too *male,* so far out of her league they might as well exist on different planets. To put it in very basic, middle-of-the-night-she-needed-sleep terms, Harrison Parker was scary as hell.

She *knew* all this, darn it.

She was on her own, doing fine, had a great career she adored, was not interested in even dating, and was very contented with the peaceful existence that she had created for herself. A life that was structured so that she was not placed in a position where she might be asked to give more than she was capable of.

So why was she sitting here like a dolt in the middle of the night drinking warm milk? It tasted yucky but she didn't have any syrup to turn it into hot chocolate…like Harrison had bought for his beautiful children when they left the library. Had he remembered to tell the waitress to add marshmallows to the creamy concoction? Surely Harrison hadn't forgotten about the promised marshmallows.

Oh, for Pete's sake, now Harrison Parker was jumping right into her milk, which had produced a nauseating gooey film on top. Her drink was now taunting her with the fact that Harrison was capable of producing delicious hot chocolate, with marshmallows, for those who went with him, instead of staying behind as she had and watching him disappear from view.

"They're coming for you, Maggie," she said, getting to her feet with a cluck of disgust. "They're on their way to tote you off to the funny farm."

She stomped to the sink, dumped the milk, rinsed the mug, then headed back to bed with a narrow-eyed, fierce determination to go to sleep the moment her head was nestled on her fluffy pillow.

But it was nearly dawn before Maggie Conrad slept.

On Sunday afternoon one of Harrison's neighbors invited the kids to join their large family for an outing to see a Disney movie at the local theater.

Ignoring the guilt that accompanied his sense of relief that the squabbling trio was going to disappear for a few hours, Harrison nearly hugged the smiling woman who came to collect his brood. He gave the mother money for admission for his three, plus added enough to buy popcorn and drinks for the whole group.

He waved as the station wagon, which appeared to hold about forty-two kids, pulled out of his driveway, then he headed for his office, eager to begin work on the project for Matt Tynan.

As he booted up the computer he was once again struck by the incredible, almost unbelievable story Matt had related to him. But it was true, all of it. Genetically engineered babies had been born and raised, each having a different superhuman power.

The project had been begun with a misplaced but sincere belief that nothing but good would be accomplished. But those with less than honorable intentions were now very much in the picture with a mind-boggling disaster to come about if they weren't stopped.

He had to get the information Matt needed, Har-

rison thought. They had to find Gideon. There was
so much at stake it was frightening. The thought
chilled him to the point that a shiver coursed throughout him.

"So get to it, Parker," he said aloud. "The kids
are happy as clams watching a movie about Clarence
the bunny or something and— Ah, hell."

Harrison sank back in the chair and dragged his
hands down his face.

No, the kids were not watching a movie about
Clarence the bunny, idiot, he thought in self-disgust.
Clarence and company belonged to Maggie Conrad.
Maggie, who was never far from his thoughts, damn
it anyway. Mysterious Maggie who seemed to
beckon to him to unravel the puzzle she represented
to him.

"Forget it," Harrison said, then typed some com-
mands into the computer.

He was soon lost in the world of cyberspace and
didn't surface until he heard the sound of his children's voices downstairs hours later. He had made
absolutely no progress whatsoever toward accom-
plishing his assignment from Matt Tynan.

Harrison shook his head slightly to bring himself
back to the reality at hand, telling himself he was
now switching his hacker hat to his daddy hat, which
was getting beat to a pulp on a daily basis.

As he pressed the necessary keys to shut down the
computer, an echo of what Matt had said about how
rough it must be for Harrison to have lost his wife
bounced around in his tired mind.

Lost his wife, he thought, as the computer hummed, then was silent as the monitor screen went dark. Lost his wife? Like a library book? A book that he'd had for so long he just took it for granted that it would always be there, but then it was gone. Took it for granted. Took *Lisa* for granted for many months preceding her death. She was there, had been for years, always would be. Wrong.

What had Lisa been thinking during those months when he'd been consumed by his work and neglected her and the children? Had Lisa tried to tell him that she was miserable and he hadn't listened? Or if she hadn't come right out and expressed her feelings, had he been so wrapped up in what *he* was doing that he'd missed the signs, the signals, that his marriage was in trouble?

Somewhere in the midst of all that tangled maze had Lisa stopped loving him because he was no longer worthy of being loved?

His children sure as hell weren't thrilled to pieces to have him for a father. Had Lisa reached the point where she no longer wanted him as a husband?

The irritating sound of the television blasting at full volume reached Harrison, rescuing him from his tormenting thoughts.

He strode from the room with the determination that the tube was going to be turned off, the kids were going to tell him all about the movie they'd seen, and he'd listen intently, giving them his undivided attention. They were going to engage in some family sharing, whether the terrible trio wanted to or not.

When Harrison reached the living room he found the children slouched on the sofa, staring at the television. He grabbed the remote from the end table and pressed the button to turn off the blaring menace.

"Hey," David said, "we were watching that, Dad."

"You spent the afternoon at the movies," Harrison said, sitting down in an easy chair. "Enough is enough." He paused. "So! Tell me about the flick you saw."

"We couldn't get into the movie because it was sold out, so we ended up at their house watching a video. It was dumb," David said. "Lame. Baby stuff. I hated it."

"Why doesn't that surprise me?" Harrison said under his breath.

"It was not baby stuff, David," Chelsey said, "and I saw you clapping your hands when the glass slipper fit Cinderella when the man came to try it on the feet of everybody in the kingdom because the prince told him to."

David lifted one shoulder in a shrug, a frown on his face.

"Cinderella, huh?" Harrison said. "That's a great fairy tale. Yep, it's a dandy. I like the part where the fairy godmother turns the pumpkin into a golden carriage so Cinderella can ride in style to the ball."

"She should have whipped out a Beemer," David

said. "Now that is style. Or maybe a classic Mustang. Yeah, a candy-apple red Mustang."

"Can it, David," Harrison said. "So, the glass slipper fit Cinderella, right, Chelsey? And she marries the handsome prince and they live happily ever after?"

"Well, yeah," Chelsey said, "until she dies and becomes an angel in heaven. Then the prince would be sad and grumpy and stuff, but they didn't show that part."

"Angel," Benny said, nodding, "in heaven."

A knot tightened in Harrison's stomach. He leaned forward, propped his elbows on his knees and clasped his hands tightly.

"Listen, guys," he said, "you mustn't think that there's a sad ending to every story. Some people, some families, really do live happily ever after."

"We didn't get to," Chelsey said.

"That doesn't mean we can't start over," Harrison said. "We can be a happy family again if we try, work at it together. I know you miss your mother, but we still have each other. That's important, worth something, don't you think?"

David narrowed his eyes. "Do *you* miss Mom?"

"Yes, of course, I do," Harrison said.

"That's bogus," David said, jumping to his feet. "How come you were never home anymore for weeks and weeks before Mom...before Mom... was...killed? How come, Dad?

"How come Mom cried a lot and didn't want to

do any fun junk with us like she did before? How come the only time she was smiling and laughing and stuff was when she did her night-out-with-the-girls thing, and she got dressed all fancy and smelled good, like flowers?''

Harrison sank back in the chair. "Your mother cried a lot?"

"She said she had allergies," Chelsey said, "but David told me and Benny that she was really crying. I don't think Mommy was doing happily ever after, Daddy.'' Her bottom lip began to tremble and she stuck her thumb in her mouth.

"Clarence the bunny did happily ever after," Benny said. "I want to go live in the woods where Clarence and Maggie are.''

"You are such a lame baby, Benny," David said, then stomped out of the living room.

"David, wait a minute," Harrison said, getting to his feet. The next sound he heard was the slamming of David's bedroom door. "Damn.''

"That's a bad word," Chelsey said, popping her thumb out of her mouth. "One time when you called here and said you were going to be very late coming home, Daddy, Mommy said damn like that, and threw the phone on the floor, and said she didn't care, and I knew she was crying for real and didn't have allergies.

"Then she called up and got a pizza to come to the house for our dinner but she didn't eat any. I ate some, but I got a tummy ache because Mommy was sad, and Benny ate some and then he threw up, and David wouldn't even come out of his room to take one bite of pizza."

Harrison sank back onto the chair. "I…I didn't know that your mother…I mean…I'm so sorry that I was away working so much of the time and…" His shoulders slumped and he shook his head. "I don't know what to say to you, Chelsey, Benny, except I'm sorry." He paused and swallowed past the lump he realized had formed in his throat. "Things are going to be different now, though. I'm here for you. I am."

Chelsey looked at him for a long moment, then poked her thumb back into her mouth.

Benny slid off the sofa and began to hop across the living room.

"I'm Clarence. I'm Clarence the bunny," he said. "I'm going to go live in the woods with Maggie. Maggie, Maggie, Maggie."

"I'll, um, go start dinner," Harrison said, rising. "Grilled cheese sandwiches. I can make those. Sure. Grilled cheese sandwiches."

Before Harrison even got to the kitchen the television once again blared and he realized that Chelsey had reached for the remote the second he'd turned his back. Benny was still hopping around the living room, chanting Maggie's name at the top of his lungs.

In the kitchen Harrison gripped the edge of the sink so tightly that his knuckles turned white as he stared unseeing out the window above the double sink.

Mom cried a lot.... The only time she was smiling was when she did her night-out-with-the-girls thing.... I don't think Mommy was doing happily ever after, Daddy...threw the phone on the floor and said she didn't care...didn't care... I knew she was crying for real...for real...for real.... I'm Clarence the bunny.... I'm going to go live in the woods with Maggie...Maggie...Maggie.... Mom cried a lot....

"Dear God," Harrison said, his voice choked with emotion, "what have I done?"

Three

Monday morning Harrison stood in the doorway of the children's room at the library that was sans kids at the moment and watched Maggie Conrad taking books from a red wagon and placing them in proper order on the shelves. She was wearing black slacks and an enormous, bright blue sweater that fell to mid-thigh.

Maggie was apparently, Harrison mused while unable to curb a smile, humming a peppy tune he couldn't hear from where he was as she was wiggling back and forth in a steady rhythm.

Was Maggie always so...so *happy?* When he was working alone in his office, *he* sure didn't feel on top of the world, bebopping around as he completed his scheduled task.

Maggie had exhibited that same kind of fun-filled energy when she'd been telling the story of Clarence the bunny, the smile on her face open, real...honest.

But then, Harrison recalled, a frown knitting his brows, her demeanor had changed the minute he'd spoken to her. She'd gotten tense, edgy, acted as though she wished he'd get the heck out of Dodge and leave her child-oriented haven. He still didn't know what he'd done to make Maggie so nervous but he was definitely going to be very careful when he spoke to her this morning.

Harrison walked slowly forward and stopped about three feet behind Maggie who had her back to him, hoping she'd somehow sense his presence. She continued to wiggle and weave and place books on the shelf.

Well, here we go, Harrison thought, then cleared his throat.

"Aak," Maggie shrieked, dropping three books and spinning around to stare at Harrison with wide eyes.

Look at that, he thought. He'd scared the bejeebers out of her. And look at that. The sweater she was wearing was the exact same shade as her big, blue eyes.

Had she chosen that sweater because it *did* match her eyes, made them more enchanting, made a man feel as though he could drown in their depths? Somehow, he didn't think so. He had a feeling the matching of the blues was a coincidence that Ms. Conrad was totally unaware of.

"I'm sorry," Harrison said, raising both hands. "I didn't mean to startle you."

"Oh, my stars," Maggie said, placing one hand on her chest. "I'm having a heart attack. You shouldn't sneak up on people, Mr. Parker."

"It's Harrison. You were so engrossed in what you were doing, Ms. Conrad, that a whole crowd of folks could have walked in here and you wouldn't have known it. But I *do* apologize for giving you a heart attack.''

''I think I'm going to live,'' Maggie said, patting her chest, then dropping her hand to her side. ''Was there something in particular you wanted this morning, Mr. Parker?''

''Harrison,'' he said, producing what he hoped was his very best smile. ''You call me Harrison and I'll call you Maggie. Okay?''

Maggie frowned. ''Why?''

''Why? Well, because it's more friendly, less formal and— Why? That's a rather unusual response to— Just call me Harrison and I'll call you Maggie.''

Maggie picked an imaginary thread from her sweater, averting her eyes from Harrison's.

''Whatever,'' she mumbled.

Oh, good grief, she thought, Harrison Parker was even more intimidating and big and male and dropdead gorgeous than she remembered him being. Remembered? Consumed by the image of him in her mind's eye was closer to the mark.

For reasons she couldn't fathom he had continually popped into her mental vision over and over again ever since he'd been there on Saturday with his children. And now here he was again, and her heart was beating like a bongo drum and her stomach was doing flip-flops. She wished there was a slew of kids in here to act as a buffer of sorts between her and the blatantly masculine Mr. Parker. Harrison.

"Well," she said, staring at the toe of one of her tennis shoes, "it was nice chatting with you but I must get back to work. So many books to put away, so little time. Have a nice day."

"Maggie," Harrison said quietly, "it's very obvious that I upset you in some way, make you...I don't know, nervous or something. If you tell me why that is, I'll stop doing whatever it is that I'm doing that I don't realize that I'm doing." He paused. "Did that make sense?"

He'd have to stop breathing and drop dead on his face to keep from throwing her off-kilter, Maggie thought miserably. She just wasn't comfortable around men in general, and especially men like Harrison Parker.

"Upset? Nervous? Me?" she said. "Don't be silly. I'm a mature twenty-seven-year-old woman, for heaven's sake, not a giddy girl who gets the vapors when in the proximity of an extremely handsome and— Erase that part. What is it that you wanted, Mr....Harrison?"

"Vapors?" Harrison said. "You know, I've never understood what that meant. What are the vapors?"

"I don't have a clue," Maggie said with a burst of laughter. "But I'm quite certain that I don't get them."

Harrison matched Maggie's smile and their gazes met for a moment that stretched into two, then three, then time lost meaning. Smiles dimmed, then disappeared to be replaced by expressions of wonder mingled with confusion. A hazy mist seemed to swirl around them, encasing them in a place where only the two of them existed.

Maggie tore her gaze from Harrison's and sank onto a small chair by one of the brightly colored little tables, her trembling legs refusing to support her for another second.

"I, um…" Harrison said, then shook his head slightly to dispel the sensuous web Maggie Conrad had woven around and through him. "Whew. Yes. Well, I'm here today because I have a proposition for you."

"What?" Maggie said, jumping to her feet.

"Oh, jeez," Harrison said. "A *business* proposition. Business. As in I hire you and I pay you money for— Cripe, I'm digging myself in deeper here. Could we start this conversation over, please? I'd prefer to take you to lunch where we could speak privately, but I'm afraid that would be cutting it close time-wise to when the van drops Benny back at the house after preschool so… Damn it, Maggie, I just want to talk to you about something."

"So talk," she said, taking a step backward, "and there's no need to swear about it."

"Is there somewhere we could sit down in human-size chairs?"

"Oh. Well, all right," she said. "My desk is over in the corner and there's a chair in front of it." She started across the room at a brisk clip.

Harrison followed her and sat in the chair opposite

the desk in question while Maggie took her place behind the desk.

Much better, she thought. There was now a nice, solid beat-up old desk between her and Harrison. Very good.

She folded her hands on top of the desk and lifted her chin.

"I'm listening," she said, then frowned. "And you're staring at me."

"I'm sorry. You're right. I was staring. This is going to bug me to death if I don't ask it for some dumb reason. Did you pick that sweater because it matches your beautiful eyes?"

"Discussion is over," Maggie said, getting to her feet.

"No, no, wait. I'm sorry. Man, all I do is apologize to you. Forget I asked about the sweater. Okay? Please? What I have to say to you is of the utmost importance, I swear it is."

Maggie narrowed her eyes, hesitated, then sat back down.

"This better be good," she said.

Harrison took a deep breath and let it out slowly.

"Maggie, I told you that I'm a widower with three children. My wife was killed by a drunk driver."

"I'm very sorry for your loss," Maggie said softly, as she fiddled with a pencil. "It must be difficult for you and your children."

"It's more than difficult, it's totally out of control," Harrison said wearily. "I told you how the kids have gone through a series of nannies and that I'm taking over now. I quit my job and am starting my own business so I can work at home. I—

"Look, I'm going to be completely honest with you, Maggie. During the months before my wife, Lisa, was killed I wasn't home much. I spent a great deal of time in Washington on special projects for the firm where I was employed and put in very long days. I hardly saw the kids or…or Lisa. I guess I felt, somewhere in my subconscious or whatever, that I would make it up to them later, that what I was doing was important and…

"Ah, hell—excuse me for swearing—there's no excuse for the way I neglected my family. I was so centered on what I was involved in that… But time ran out, and Lisa was killed and now my kids act like I'm a stranger who is attempting to perform in the role of their father. I've made a royal mess of everything."

"I see." Maggie looked up at Harrison quickly, then redirected her attention to the pencil.

"I can't begin to tell you," Harrison went on, "what it meant to me to see my children so free with their emotions, so normal, happy and enthused while they were listening to you tell the story about Clarence.

"Then you hugged them. You hugged them and they hugged you back. They don't allow me to hug or kiss them, Maggie. I think they blame me somehow for their not having their mother anymore, and

I know for a fact that they feel I made Lisa very unhappy during those months I was an absentee husband and father.''

"Have you considered getting counseling for the children, for all of you?" Maggie said, finally looking directly at Harrison.

"Oh, yeah, I went that route, but they just sat there and refused to respond. Now Chelsey is sucking her thumb, which she hasn't done since she was in diapers. Benny hardly speaks. David is so angry he... But with you? Interacting with you? They're children again, the kids I remember them being. I need your help. I need you, Maggie.''

Something strange and warm and wonderful suffused Maggie as she listened to Harrison's heartfelt words, heard the sincerity and, yes, the pain ringing in his voice.

I need you, Maggie.

Not once, she thought, in her entire life had anyone said that to her. Oh, her parents had loved her, had been the best mother and father a child could ever hope to have. But they didn't *need* her as she, little Maggie growing up, had needed them.

And the one disastrous relationship she'd had with a man five years ago? Larry hadn't *needed* her, he'd *used* her, taken advantage of her lack of sophistication and experience until he'd grown bored with her unworldliness and walked out of her life without a backward glance, leaving her with a shattered heart.

I need you, Maggie.

"I don't quite understand," she said, her voice trembling slightly. "How can I possibly help you and the situation you're in with your children beyond welcoming them here for story hour on Saturdays?"

Harrison leaned forward, folding his arms on the top of the desk.

"You could be the kids' nanny, per se," he said. "I realize you have a job here at the library, but you could come to the house after you're finished for the day. Fix dinner, spend the evening, tuck them in bed. They'd go to sleep as innocent, happy children should, instead of the angry, upset kids they are. It would be a start toward their healing, toward their hopefully forgiving me for not being the kind of father I should have been."

Maggie frowned. "You're talking about my putting in many hours at your home after working a full day here. I don't see how I could keep up a pace like that."

Harrison blurted out the amount of money he would be willing to pay Maggie and her breath caught.

"You're joking," she said.

"No, I'm desperate."

"I could pay off my college student loans in a fraction of the time it will take me now and— No, no, money isn't the issue. Yes, it is. Who am I kidding? I'm just scraping by because of the loans I'm buried under. The thing is, I'm afraid that something would suffer. Either my work here, or my ability to

be what I should be for your children. I'm very
tempted, Harrison, I won't pretend that I'm not,
but..." She shook her head.

"Okay, let's compromise," he said quickly. "I
just got an assignment from a friend who...
It's...a...a government project, top-secret thing, that
is going to take many hours for me to accomplish. I
need the hours the kids are in school to work on other
jobs I've contracted for and intended to concentrate
on this new assignment after they went to bed each
night.

"But the thing is, I'm so wiped out by the time I
fight the battles with those kids before they go to bed
that I'm useless. I'll never be able to complete what
I must, what is of extreme importance that I do. Suppose we agree that you take us on for the duration
of that project."

"How long do you think that would be?"

"I don't know for sure," he said. "Weeks? A couple of months? Maybe it won't be that long if I can
tackle it at night with my head on straight."

Maggie nodded slowly. "When were you thinking
of me starting?"

"Today. Well, this evening really, after you get
off work here. But if that's too soon, just say so. Just
don't say no. Please."

I need you, Maggie.

Harrison's words echoed once again in Maggie's
mind.

This was crazy, she thought. She gave her job at

the library her all, often dragged herself home so exhausted it took the last ounce of energy she had to fix herself a simple dinner. But if she could reach deep within herself for a reserve that surely must be there somewhere, she could be free of the huge debts and...

And she could make those beautiful, sad and unhappy children smile.

Oh, but, no, she didn't want to spend hours under the same roof with Harrison Parker every evening. She became a blithering idiot, a befuddled mess, whenever she was close to him and that was on *her* turf, here in the safe and comforting room she'd created, her world of fantasy and fun.

But those children had allowed her to hug them and Harrison said they refused his attempts to hold and kiss them. That was so sad, so wrong.

I need you, Maggie.

Yes, he did. No, not for himself. Not a man saying that to a woman. He *needed* her to interact with his brokenhearted, disillusioned children, who were being swallowed up by the dark gloom of their sorrow and anger when they should be carefree and laughing in the bright sunshine that every child deserved to bask in.

"Maggie?"

"Yes, all right, Harrison, I accept your...proposition with the understanding that it's only for as long as you are working on the special project you spoke of. And with the provision that if I find it's just too exhausting to work two jobs, then our agreement will end, even if you're still involved in that assignment.''

Harrison closed his eyes for a moment and drew a deep breath, letting it out slowly. He opened his eyes again and smiled.

''Thank you,'' he said, getting to his feet. ''That's not big enough, doesn't begin to cut it, but it's all I have. Thank you, Maggie. When do you want to start?''

''I'll be there this evening at five-thirty,'' she said. ''I'll need your address, of course, and... Do you have food in the house that I can use to prepare dinner?''

''I bought all kinds of stuff,'' he said, ''but then realized I didn't know how to fix a decent meal from what I got.'' He wrote the address on a memo pad on the desk.

''Fine,'' Maggie said, rising. ''I'll see you this evening then.''

Harrison extended his hand. ''Until this evening.''

Maggie looked at Harrison's hand, his face, then back at his hand. She lifted her right hand and placed it in his, immediately feeling a jolt of heat travel up her arm and across her breasts. She snatched her hand away.

''I must get back to work,'' she said.

''Sure. You bet. Thanks again.''

Harrison strode from the room and Maggie sank back onto her chair as she watched him go. She lifted her right hand for a moment, stared at it and told herself firmly that she did not still feel the heat from Harrison's strong but gentle hand.

"Oh, Maggie," she said, pressing her hands to her flushed cheeks, "you have got to be out of your mind." She sighed. "But I guess the big issue at the moment is...what's for dinner?"

Harrison's euphoric mood when he left the library was blown away by a flat tire on his SUV on the way home. He knew he was racing the clock, had to be there when Benny was dropped off. His attempt to rush to change the tire resulted in him turning into a fumble fingers, causing the chore to take twice as long as it normally would.

He drove above the speed limit and arrived to find a note taped to the front door of the house saying that Benny was next door. He ran across the connecting lawns and knocked on the door, which was opened by an attractive woman in her mid-thirties.

"You have Benny, Justine?" Harrison said.

"Come on in, Harrison," Justine said, frowning as she stepped back to allow him room to enter.

"Where is he?" Harrison said, as Justine closed the door. "Is he all right? I had a flat tire and..."

"Ever heard of cell phones?" Justine said. "You could have called me and I would have been waiting for Benny at your house. As it is, Harrison, he was nearly hysterical by the time he came over here. He waited and waited for you, was so cold and scared and…'' She shook her head.

"I left my cell phone on my desk at the house,'' Harrison said, dragging one hand through his hair. "Man, every time I turn around I mess something up. I had no idea it was so complicated to keep things running smoothly in a house. Lisa always made it seem so easy.''

"A fact you took for granted.'' Justine frowned. "I'm sorry. I shouldn't have said that. I fed Benny some lunch and he fell asleep on the sofa in the family room. I'll bring him home when he wakes up.''

"Thank you,'' Harrison said. "I appreciate everything you did for him.'' He paused. "Justine, back up to what you said about my taking for granted what Lisa did to maintain order in our house. What you're really saying is that I took Lisa herself for granted. Right?''

"There's no point in discussing it now, Harrison,'' Justine said. "Lisa is gone. She was my best friend and I still miss her so much. Sometimes I start toward the door to go over and see if she has a pot of coffee on and then it hits me again…she isn't there.''

"She isn't there now,'' Harrison said quietly, "and I wasn't there for months before she was killed.''

"No, you weren't, but what's done is done. There's no point in going down the 'if only' road, Harrison. It won't change anything.''

"The kids…the kids made it clear that their

mother was very unhappy because I wasn't home much. Is that true, Justine?''

"Harrison, don't do this," she said.

"Please. I have to know."

Justine sighed. "Yes. Lisa was... All right, you want to know so here it is. Lisa was miserable, so unhappy it just broke my heart."

"I..."

"The night she was killed she came over here to get me because it was our girls' night out, as we called it. There were four of us who got together once a month for dinner and— You know that part.

"I had a bad cold and decided I just wasn't up to going out. If I had gone I probably wouldn't be standing here talking to you right now. I would no doubt have been killed when that drunk driver hit Lisa's car and...I think I'm suffering from survivor's guilt as well as missing Lisa so very much.

"Anyway, Harrison, that night Lisa told me before she left here that she couldn't go on any longer acting as a single parent when she was supposedly married. She felt she was in limbo, married but with a husband who was never home, that she wasn't free to move forward with her life. She...she had decided to tell you she... Harrison, what is the point of this?''

"Go on," he said, a pulse beating wildly in his temple.

"She was going to tell you she wanted a divorce," Justine said, then tears filled her eyes. "She said...she said, 'I wonder when it happened, Justine?

I wonder when Harrison and I stopped loving each other.'"

"My God," Harrison whispered, feeling the color drain from his face. "Lisa didn't love me anymore?"

"Oh, don't you dare get on a pity trip, Harrison Parker," Justine said, swiping two tears from her cheeks. "I can see it now. 'My dear dead wife didn't love me and I didn't know that and blah, blah, blah.'

"Well, mister, I don't think you loved Lisa, either, and she was convinced that you didn't. It was a given, Harrison, a done deal, your marriage was over, but for some reason Lisa wanted to know when you two stopped loving each other. She never got an answer to that question, did she? But I guess it really doesn't matter."

"I don't...I don't know what to say," Harrison said, his voice raspy.

"Just don't stand there and say that you loved Lisa with every breath in your body, or some such corny thing, because I won't buy it."

"I should have been home more. I should have—"

"No. No. No," Justine said, shaking her head. "Don't you get it, Harrison? Your working those ridiculous hours didn't cause your marriage to fall apart. They were the product of a marriage that was already over. You had nothing to come home to except the kids. Lisa knew that. She was hanging on because of the kids."

"She...she didn't care if I was there, or not," Harrison said, a chill coursing through him. "Is that what you're saying, Justine?"

"I... Damn it, yes, that's exactly what I'm saying. Maybe this is good. I don't know, but at least it's all out in the open now. What were you really grieving for all those months you ignored your children, Harrison? Lisa's death? Or the death of your marriage that had ended many, many months before she died?

"You don't miss her, you miss what you had together a long time ago. You two were just going through the motions for the sake of the kids without even discussing it. But Lisa was done, finished living out a sham, a charade."

"She was going to tell me she wanted a divorce," Harrison said, his voice seeming to come from a faraway place.

"Yes."

"Maybe I knew that. Maybe I worked those long hours so I wouldn't have to hear Lisa say that she... When did we stop loving each other? I don't know, Justine."

"You had to have been just as unhappy as Lisa was," Justine said gently, "but you buried yourself in work rather than face the truth. Well, there's nowhere to hide from it any longer, Harrison. Deal with it. Then move heaven and earth to put your shattered children back together."

Sudden tears closed Harrison's throat and he could only nod. He gripped Justine's shoulders, kissed her on the forehead, then moved around her and left the house.

Not certain how he had gotten there, Harrison found himself in the bedroom he had shared with Lisa. He picked up a frame from the top of his dresser and stared at the photograph taken on the day they were married.

They looked so happy, so filled with joy, he thought. What hopes and dreams they had for their future, for their happily ever after. When had it started to fall apart? Oh, God, when had they stopped loving each other?

"I'm sorry, Lisa," Harrison said, his voice gritty with emotion. "You'd probably say that to me, too, wouldn't you? I'm sorry, Harrison. Yeah. We took those vows and we're both to blame for breaking them. We didn't even make it to 'until death do us part,' did we? I'm just so damn sorry."

Harrison dropped the frame into the trash basket next to the dresser, flinching as he heard the glass break.

He'd failed as a husband, he thought, not even attempting to stop the flow of tears that ran down his face. He'd failed, and there was no way to turn back the clock and change things.

And he'd failed as a father.

But, by damn, he was being given another chance in that role. He had three beautiful miracles created with a fine, decent woman he had once loved beyond measure. He had three children...who hated him.

Well, that was going to change...somehow. Whatever it took, whatever he had to do, he would regain the love of his children, make them believe and trust in him again, love him again. There would be laughter singing through this home...somehow. Benny, Chelsey, David were his life now, his focus, his purpose, his reason for being. The damage done had to be repaired...somehow.

And now he had help with his mission.

Because now there was Maggie.

Four

For the next hour Harrison sat in front of the computer in his office and replayed over and over in his mind his conversation with Justine.

Conversation, he finally thought with a shake of his head. A conversation was idle chitchat about the latest antics of kids, the condition of the stock market, and the weather.

What he'd taken part in with Justine was stark, a revealing of cold, hard facts that he'd been running from for a very long time. That Lisa had been going to ask him for a divorce hurt deeply, yet he had to admit that he'd known it was coming. So, if he didn't arrive home at a decent hour Lisa couldn't corner him and say the words that would end the lifestyle he'd had for the past dozen years.

He would have been a weekend father, Harrison mused. Picking up the kids, taking them to the park, the zoo, the movies, then delivering them home at the designated hour before returning to wherever he had chosen to live. Alone.

Man, what a bleak picture that painted in his mind, and one he'd postponed having become reality by refusing to be available. He was a coward on top of all his other sins.

"Ah, hell," Harrison said, "enough of this."

There was no point in rehashing the mess his life was in. What was important was the positive steps he was taking to set things to rights with his children.

Maggie.

She never did answer his question about whether she'd purposely bought that blue sweater because it matched her eyes. He'd still bet a buck that she hadn't because she didn't seem like the type who—

"Work," Harrison said. "Get to work and accomplish something while Benny is napping. Hear that, Parker? Get to work."

Fifteen minutes later Justine delivered a grumpy Benny into Harrison's care, and fifteen minutes after that Chelsey and David got off the school bus, ran into the house and demanded to know what they could have for a snack.

Harrison toyed with the idea of telling the kids about Maggie's pending arrival, then decided not to. He was, he admitted to himself, afraid she'd think it over, then telephone to say she'd changed her mind. He was the bad guy often enough in the eyes of his children without promising them the company of magical Maggie Conrad, then not producing her.

After the kids had their snack, Harrison decided, they'd all pitch in together and straighten up the house, which was a cluttered mess, to reduce the risk of Maggie taking one look around and hightailing it back out the door.

Just as Harrison was about to assign chores, he received a long-distance call from one of his clients and ended up in his office on the telephone for almost two hours. He had just returned to the living room when the doorbell rang, causing him to groan as he looked at his watch.

That was Maggie, he thought, glancing at the disaster of a living room. Great. Just dandy.

"Turn that television down," Harrison said, as he strode toward the front door.

David, Chelsey and Benny didn't pay the least bit of attention to him.

Harrison opened the door and stepped back to make space for Maggie to enter.

"Hi," he said, speaking loudly to be heard over the blaring television. "I'm glad you're here."

Maggie opened her mouth to reply to Harrison's greeting, then snapped it closed again as she swept her wide-eyed gaze over the scene before her.

Not only was the television turned to a volume loud enough to shatter windows, there were dirty dishes littering the end tables and coffee table. Clothes and toys were scattered across the carpet. Benny was jumping on the sofa in a steady rhythm, David was chomping on potato chips from the bag in his hand and Chelsey was sitting on the floor looking into a mirror on the coffee table as she applied a thick layer of toy makeup to her tiny face.

"You're in deep, deep trouble here," Maggie said, shaking her head.

"In spades," Harrison said with a weary sigh.

Maggie set a tote bag on a chair, removed her coat and placed it across the top of the chair, then marched forward to turn off the television. She then stood directly in front of the screen.

"Maggie?" David said, jerking upward from his slouched position so quickly that he spilled half the bag of chips on the carpet.

"Maggie, Maggie, Maggie," Benny said, in time to three bounces on the sofa.

"Hi, Maggie," Chelsey said. "See my face? I'm a beautiful princess. Why are you here? We're glad you came, but how come you did?"

"I didn't tell them that you..." Harrison started, then shrugged.

"I see," Maggie said. "Well, kiddies, I'm here to help out a bit. Cool, huh?"

"Way cool," David said. "Are you going to cook dinner instead of my dad?"

"Yes, I am," Maggie said, nodding.

"Great," David said. "I need to watch my favorite show on TV now, though. Tell me when you want me to wash my hands for dinner and I'll scrub them really clean."

"Well, I'm certainly glad to hear that you'll be eating with clean hands, David," Maggie said, "but before that can happen there are things to be done."

"Like what?" David said. "My show is on."

"Your show is off," Maggie said. "This television set just became invisible until I say it's available. Now then, let's begin, shall we? David, put that bag of chips away, then get the vacuum and sweep up all those you dropped on the floor. Chelsey, go wash your face and wherever you found the makeup, return it to that spot. Benny, stop jumping on the sofa right now."

A grin broke across Harrison's face as he saw the shocked expressions on the children's faces.

Talk about coming in and taking charge, he thought. Maggie Conrad was something else.

"Harrison," Maggie said, "you're to collect all these dirty dishes, scrape and rinse them, and put them in the dishwasher if you have one."

Harrison's smile slid right off his chin.

"Each of you retrieve your own toys and clothes from the floor," Maggie went on. "Clothes go in the laundry, toys in their proper place in your rooms. Anything left on the floor will be considered unwanted and will go in the trash. Any questions? No? Okay. I'll go start dinner while you tend to your chores."

Harrison stared in amazement as the children scrambled to begin their assignments.

"Harrison?" Maggie said. "It would appear that you're the only one not following instructions."

"What?" he said. "Oh. Right. Dirty dishes. I'm on it, Maggie."

"Good," she said, starting across the room.

"Maggie?" Harrison said.

She stopped and looked back at him over one shoulder.

"Yes, Harrison?"

"Thank you," he said, smiling.

"For being a bossy shrew?" she said, laughing. "I was winging it but, hey, whatever works. At least I didn't ask anyone to salute me."

"I think my kids would have been happy to salute, turn cartwheels, anything you asked of them."

"Today," she said, still smiling. "While I'm a novelty. I fully expect some mutiny before we're finished here, but I won't worry about that now. I'm off to see what I can produce for dinner. I assume I'm heading in the direction of the kitchen?"

"Yes, you are," Harrison said, then began to pick up the dishes while making no attempt to hide his smile that remained firmly in place.

An hour later the group sat down at the table and began to consume a meal of hamburgers, country fries, corn on the cob and a lettuce and tomato salad.

"Super," David said, as he chewed a big bite of hamburger.

"Please don't talk with your mouth full, David," Maggie said pleasantly.

"'kay," he said.

"Are you going to live with us forever, Maggie?" Benny said.

"I'm not going to live with you at all, sweetheart," Maggie said. "I'll just be here in the evenings for a while."

"If you want to live with us forever," Benny said, "you can sleep in my bed with me." He frowned. "Maybe you should sleep in my dad's bed with him 'cause his bed is bigger than mine. Yeah. That would be good."

She was blushing, Maggie thought, closing her eyes for a mortifying moment. Twenty-seven years old and she was blushing because of an innocent remark made by a heart-stealing little boy.

"Are you going to comment on Benny's plan, Maggie?" Harrison said, grinning.

Maggie snapped her head around and glared at him.

"Don't push it, Harrison," she said, causing him to hoot with laughter.

"What's funny?" Benny said, obviously confused.

"Just eat your dinner, sport," Harrison said. Benny was chattering like a magpie and it was music to his daddy's ears. "Maggie really fixed us a fine dinner here."

"Mom never let us have hamburgers for dinner," David said. "She said they were just for lunch on Saturday sometimes. Maybe we shouldn't eat this stuff."

"Hey," Harrison said, frowning. "Just clean your plate and—"

"David," Maggie interrupted, "I respect your mother's views on hamburgers for dinner but, honey, your mother isn't here. Things have changed, David, and you, all of you, have to go with the flow. It won't always be easy to do that, but we'll muddle through. You've just about finished that hamburger. Would you like another one?''

David stared at Maggie for a long moment, while Harrison held his breath.

"Yes," David said finally, and Harrison drew some much needed air into his lungs.

"Yes? Yes what?" Maggie said.

"Yes, please, I'd like another hamburger, Maggie," David said.

"Coming right up," Maggie said, getting to her feet. "Harrison, how about you?"

"Yes, please, Maggie," he said, smiling. "I'd like another hamburger, too."

The meal was finished with lively conversation that jumped from one topic to the next with Maggie prompting everyone to take part.

Benny said that his friend Joey had brought worms from his worm aquarium in a can to school and the teacher made him put them outside.

Chelsey announced that two boys got caught peeking in the girls' bathroom and they had to go to the principal's office.

David shared the fact that he'd made three free throws while playing basketball in P.E.

And Harrison drank in the sound of his children's voices speaking in animated tones sprinkled with laughter.

Ice cream was polished off for dessert, then Maggie told everyone to carry their dishes to the counter.

"Okay, here's the scoop," she said. "David, do you have homework?"

"Well, yeah, but—"

"Fine. Bring it to the table now and get started. Benny, it's a bubble bath for you. Chelsey, you help your father put the food away, then you'll have your bath. Harrison, you're in charge of loading the dishwasher. Come on, Benny bug, let's hit the suds."

Harrison watched as Benny put his little hand in Maggie's offered one and they left the kitchen.

Magical Maggie, he mused.

"Um, Dad?" David said.

"What?" Harrison said, directing his attention to David.

"I think we'd better get it in gear, do what Maggie told us to. I don't think she's into saying things twice, you know what I mean?"

"Good point," Harrison said, getting to his feet.

"Dad?" David said. "Do you think Mom would be mad that we had hamburgers for dinner?"

"No, David," Harrison said quietly, "I believe that Mom would realize that Maggie is right. Things have changed, and we need to go with that."

"'kay," David said, nodding. "I gotta get my homework."

"Come on, Chelsey," Harrison said, "you're helping me put stuff away."

"I like Maggie a whole bunch," Chelsey said, picking up the mustard jar.

Harrison stared at the doorway that Maggie had disappeared through holding Benny's tiny hand securely in hers.

"I like Maggie a whole bunch, too, Chelsey," he said. "She's...well, she's a very special lady."

After Harrison finished cleaning the kitchen he made a fire in the hearth in the living room, something he hadn't bothered to do yet that winter. The crackling flames cast a rosy glow over the room. He stared at the mesmerizing flames, thinking yet again about what Justine had told him.

He was a jumbled mess of emotions, he thought. A part of him felt the pain of a very deep sorrow over the death of his marriage that was separate and apart from his sadness that Lisa had died so young and his children no longer had a mother.

Lisa has been the mother of his children, but at some point in their lives she was no longer his loving wife, because he was not a husband who deserved that kind of love and loyalty.

He didn't have what it took, the depth, the understanding, to be an equal partner, a soul mate, the other half of a couple who could weather whatever storms came their way. Until death parted them.

While he was registering a sense of closure about losing Lisa, he was having a difficult time accepting his flaws, his inadequacies. He was attempting, and failing, to square off against the fact that he could never measure up, give enough, be enough for a woman. He could never again be a husband because he didn't know how to fulfill that role. He had failed.

He was a lousy father, too, Harrison mused, but, by damn, whatever it required, whatever he had to do, he was going to learn how to perform in that role the way a man should. He'd watch Maggie, listen to her, as she interacted with his kids, hope and pray that he had what it took to give his children a reason to love him, believe in him, trust him not to let them down...again.

Then someday David, Chelsey and Benny would be up and grown, head out into the world to discover their place and their destiny.

And he would be left behind...alone.

God, what a bleak picture that was in his mind's eye. He'd envisioned growing old with Lisa, enjoying their grandchildren when they came to visit, traveling, being just the two of them again as they'd been in the beginning.

When they'd been in love.

But even if Lisa hadn't been killed, that scenario wouldn't have come to be. She had stopped loving him, and he hadn't loved her the way he should because he just didn't know how. Oh, yeah, he was a failure in that arena and it was a bitter pill to swallow.

"Can we toast marshmallows in the fire, Daddy?" Chelsey said, bringing Harrison from his tangled and tormented thoughts. She and Benny had entered the living room.

"No, sweetheart," he said, "that's not something you do inside a house. It's too dangerous. That's for when you're out camping and have a special kind of fire."

Chelsey frowned. "But we never go camping. I've never had a toasted marshmallow in my whole life long."

"I don't know the first thing about camping," Harrison said. "Maybe I could read about it in a book or something and we could give it a try in the summer."

"Well, no, that's okay," Chelsey said. "My friend Jessica said that when you go camping you have to go potty by a bush and I don't think that sounds so good."

"You've got a point there," Harrison said, laughing. "You sure look pretty in your nightie."

"I had bubbles in my bath," Chelsey said, "then Maggie put powder on my tummy. It was Mommy's powder that she told me never to touch but Maggie said it would be okay as long as I didn't use it when Maggie wasn't here."

"That's fine," Harrison said. "Hey, Benny, you look snug as a bunny in your blanket sleepers."

"They're blue," Benny said. "I know all my colors now. Blue is a boy color."

"Oh, I don't know about that," Harrison said. "Maggie's eyes are blue and she isn't a boy." Not even close. She was a lovely, intriguing, breath-of-fresh-air woman. She was magical Maggie. "I think blue belongs to both boys *and* girls."

"Story time," Maggie said, coming into the room. "I brought a book with me, or I can read you one of yours. I have *The Velveteen Rabbit* in my tote bag."

David arrived in pajamas and robe.

"That's a baby story," he said.

"Then don't listen to it," Maggie said pleasantly.

"Can I watch TV?" David said.

"Nope," Maggie said. "This is story time, and we have a marvelous fire to keep us toasty warm here in the reading room."

"Well, fine," David said, an angry edge to his voice. "I'll just go to my room and…do stuff."

"Okay," Maggie said, taking the book from her tote bag. "Have fun."

"I will," David snapped, but didn't move from where he was standing.

Maggie settled onto the sofa, and Benny and Chelsey climbed up to sit on either side of her.

"You don't have room for me anyway," David said. "So I'm going."

Maggie scooped Benny onto her lap. "Now there's room, David. Your choice." She opened the book. "Well, let's see what this rabbit has to teach us."

"It's totally lame," David said, walking slowly toward the sofa.

"Maybe," Harrison said, settling into a recliner. "But I want to hear this story."

"Aren't you going to work on your project?" Maggie said, looking over at him.

"Oh," he said. "Well, sure, yeah...later. I want to be available to tuck these guys in. Go ahead with the story, Maggie."

"Whatever," David said, slouching onto the spot that Benny had vacated.

As Maggie began to read, Harrison felt himself relax, felt his tense muscles unwind for the first time in longer than he could remember.

If someone took a photograph of this scene, he thought, they'd believe they were looking at a picture of a family coming together to hear a wondrous story in front of a warming fire at day's end. It would appear like a perfect postcard. Mother, father, children...sharing and caring.

He could not remember ever doing something like this with Lisa. When he was home, he said good night to the kids, while sitting in this very chair, then she went with them to hear their prayers and that was that.

This, he thought, sweeping his gaze over the entire room and its occupants, was nice. Really, really nice. The way it should be.

Maggie read on.

"Whoa," David said. "They're going to dump the rabbit just because the kid breathed his germs on it or something? That's cold. What's the matter with that jerk? He should go rescue his rabbit."

Harrison stifled a chuckle.

"Well, let's see what happens," Maggie said.

At the end of the story all three Parker children cheered for the rabbit who had become real because it was loved.

"Cool," David said.

"I like that story," Chelsey said.

"Am I real, Maggie?" Benny said.

"Oh, yes, Benny bug, you are real," she said, smiling at him, "because you are very, very loved. Now it's off to bed with you three."

"I don't go to bed when the babies do," David said.

"Yes, you do," Maggie said. "You can read for a while if you like, though."

"Oh, well, okay then," David said.

"Harrison," Maggie said, "your troops are ready to be tucked in. Good night, good night, good night," she added, hugging each of the children in turn.

"Aren't you coming to tuck us in?" Chelsey said. "And hear our prayers?"

"No, that's your daddy's job," Maggie said. "Off you go. I'll see you tomorrow evening."

"I don't want Daddy to tuck me in," Chelsey said. "I want you to do it, Maggie."

"No, Chelsey," Maggie said firmly. "You can have your daddy do it, or you can put yourself to bed. Take your pick."

Harrison got to his feet and extended one hand toward Chelsey, his heart thundering in his chest.

Please, baby girl, he thought. Give me a chance. Please, Chelsey.

Chelsey slid off the sofa, looked at Maggie, her daddy, poked her thumb in her mouth, took it out again, then crossed the room and placed her little hand in Harrison's big one.

"Yes," Maggie whispered.

"Yes," Harrison said softly, meeting Maggie's gaze for a long moment.

When Harrison returned to the living room, Maggie wasn't there, but he could hear noise coming from the kitchen and went to investigate.

"All tucked in?" Maggie said, when he entered the kitchen.

"Yes," Harrison said. "I didn't push it by trying to hug or kiss any of them, but I heard their prayers and straightened the blankets around them."

"It's a start, Harrison," Maggie said, smiling. "A very good one."

Harrison nodded.

"So, okay, I've set the table for breakfast," Maggie said. "Bowls for cereal, plates for toast, glasses for milk and juice."

"Thank you," Harrison said. "And thank you for a great dinner and a super evening and—"

"Enough, enough," she said, smiling. "I thoroughly enjoyed myself." She frowned. "There's no need to thank me, anyway, Harrison, because I'm doing what you're paying me to do."

"No, there's no way to put a price tag on your

teaching me how to be a decent father,'' he said. ''I've got a lot to learn. I'll have to live with the fact that I'm a failure, always would be, in the role of husband, but I'm going to do everything within my power to become a good dad…with your help.''

Maggie frowned and cocked her head slightly to one side. ''What makes you believe that you are destined to be a failure as a hus— Never mind. I'm sorry. It's none of my business. I must go. It's been a long day.''

Don't go, Harrison thought suddenly. Not yet, Maggie. They could sit by the fire for a while, talk, get to know each other better and… Ah, hell, Parker, knock it off.

''Right,'' he said. ''I'm headed for my office and some solid hours of work on that special project. I ought to be able to accomplish something tonight since I haven't fought the wars with the Parker pack this evening.'' He chuckled. ''You sure pushed David's buttons like a pro about listening to the lame, baby story. You're really something, Maggie. Something very rare, very special.''

She couldn't breathe, Maggie thought frantically. The kitchen seemed to have shrunk in size, to be filled to overflowing by Harrison's presence, his masculinity, the rich timbre of his voice and the warming caress of the lovely words he was saying to her. She could not breathe.

''I…'' she said, then drew a shuddering breath. ''I have to go. I'm tired. Yes. Exhausted. I'll be back tomorrow evening. I'll let myself out, Harrison.

Don't feel you have to see me to the door. Please. Bye.''

Maggie scooted around Harrison, then hurried from the room. Harrison turned and watched her go, soon hearing the click of the front door closing behind her.

He'd done it again, he thought incredulously, dragging one hand through his hair. When the kids were there Maggie had been relaxed, her smiles and laughter never far away, her motherly instincts sharp and focused.

But the very second she was alone with him? He did something to frighten her, cause her to get flustered, nervous, nearly fall over her own feet to get away from him. What was he doing wrong in regard to Maggie Conrad?

"Well, damn it, isn't this just the greatest newsflash I've ever had?" Harrison said aloud.

Not only was he a failure in the husband material category, he was a zero when it came to interacting with women in general. No, forget women in general. He wanted to know why he upset *Maggie* so much. He wanted to know why and then fix it.

He didn't understand why it was important to him, he really didn't, but he couldn't stand to see her act like a delicate, skittish fawn when she was alone with him.

Why did it matter?

Hell, he didn't know.

It just did.

Five

Tuesday and Wednesday evenings followed the same pattern as Monday night, except for the fact that the house had been picked up before Maggie's arrival.

Harrison was very aware that Benny had little to say after preschool, Chelsey sucked her thumb once she'd consumed her after-school snack and David either went to his room or slouched on the sofa to watch TV. Any attempt on Harrison's part to engage the trio in conversation was ignored.

But the minute he said it was time to shape up the place before Maggie came, the children jumped to their feet and cooperated with no fuss.

It was better than nothing, Harrison thought, but it sure shouted the message that the Parker children had little use for their father. Maggie, too, continued to seem very uncomfortable around him once the kids were in bed. She rattled off instructions for breakfast, then made a beeline for the door.

On Thursday night Harrison once again found Maggie in the kitchen setting the table for breakfast the next morning after he had listened to the kids' prayers.

"All set," Maggie said, then turned to look at Harrison. "I wanted to discuss tomorrow with you, Harrison."

"Tomorrow? Well, sure," he said. "Let's go in by the fire."

"It won't take that long," Maggie said. "I just thought…"

"No sense in wasting a warm, crackling fire," he said, then strode from the kitchen.

"Oh," Maggie said to no one.

Back in the living room Harrison sat in his usual chair and Maggie settled onto the sofa where the story of the night had been *Black Beauty.*

"A person can totally lose track of time when they stare into the flames of a fire in the hearth," Harrison said, looking at the leaping flames for a moment, then meeting Maggie's gaze. "Did you ever notice that?"

"I haven't been around fires in the hearth that much to know," Maggie said. "Anyway, about tomorrow…"

"You don't have a fireplace wherever it is you're living?"

"No, I rent a guest house behind a large home. My little place is very cozy but it doesn't have a fireplace. We didn't have one while I growing up, either, so…" Maggie shrugged. "Tomorrow is Friday and—"

"You told the kids that your parents are angels in heaven," Harrison said, interrupting her again. "You're awfully young to have lost your folks."

"I was a late-in-life surprise," Maggie said, "and my parents also had health problems as they grew older. They were wonderful and I still miss them very much especially since I don't have any other relatives, no extended family." She paused. "Do your children have grandparents?"

"No," Harrison said. "Lisa's father died when she was a child, and her mother became ill and died about a year after Lisa and I were married. My folks passed away within months of each other when David was a baby. Lisa and I were both only children so I'm all the kids have, which obviously doesn't thrill the socks off of them."

"You have to be patient, Harrison," Maggie said. "They're very animated during dinner and it's understood that you're going to tuck them in. You're making progress reconnecting with them."

"They don't respond to me at all when you're not here, Maggie," Harrison said, shaking his head. "Benny clams up, Chelsey sucks her thumb, David broods. The smiles appear when you arrive."

"Give it time," she said. "They'll come to see that you're here for them, that you won't grow tired of them and start disappearing every evening, working long hours and what have you. They're protecting themselves and that's understandable. They'll realize that they have a father who is focused on them and loves them very much, you'll see."

"I hope you're right. I *pray* you're right," Harrison said. "They're all I have, all I'll *ever* have.

Heaven knows I'll never remarry." He paused. "Why aren't you married, Maggie?"

"Wait a minute," she said, frowning. "Back up here. A few nights ago you said you had been a failure as a husband and always would fail in that role, or something close to that. It's none of my business, Harrison, but I'm witnessing how hard you're trying to be a good father. It's difficult for me to believe that you couldn't be a devoted and loving husband as well."

Harrison shook his head. "I'm in the process of learning how to be a decent father, Maggie. Think about that. David is ten years old, for Pete's sake, and has little use for me. The only saving grace here is that I'm getting another chance at being a father who is worthy of receiving the love of his children.

"Maggie, I was a lousy husband as well as a crummy father. Lisa was about to ask me for a divorce when she was killed. I knew that, somewhere deep inside me, and ran from that truth by working late and making it impossible for her to confront me, tell me. I won't get a second chance in the husband role because I don't have a clue about how to love a woman the way I should. I don't believe I'm capable of doing that."

"You could learn, just as you're learning how to be a proper father."

"No," Harrison said. "I have a major flaw in my role as a man to a woman and I'm trying to accept that. You of all people should realize that by now."

"Me?"

"Well, cripe, Maggie, every time we're alone you get so edgy, so nervous, I feel like Jack the Ripper. I can't even carry on a casual conversation with a woman, with you, without doing something that makes you want to put as much distance between us as you possibly can. That sure doesn't say much for my ability to interact with women, does it? Hell, no. Excuse me for swearing."

"Oh, Harrison, you're not being fair to yourself. The fact that you…jangle me, or whatever, is *my* flaw, *my* fault. You haven't done one thing wrong when we've been…alone together."

Harrison got to his feet and went to the hearth, staring into the flames for a long moment before turning to look at Maggie again.

"Why?" he said quietly. "Why do I upset you?"

"It's just a combination of things," Maggie said, averting her eyes from Harrison's intense gaze. She fiddled with the waistband of her baggy sweater. "My parents were older, we lived a very quiet, sedate life. I was shy, didn't have many friends, never dated in high school.

"The one relationship I had years ago with a man ended in disaster and I just feel safer alone, on my own. I'm quite contented with my life as it is. I'm just…just not comfortable around men, adults in general, as a matter of fact. It's nothing personal, Harrison."

"I see," he said slowly. "It seems to me that you

have something that needs work, just as I do in my role of father, and this is a perfect opportunity for you to get started.''

Maggie's head snapped up and she looked at Harrison.

"What do you mean?" she said, frowning.

"You need to move past your fear—or whatever you want to call it—of adults, of men in particular. I'm here. I'm a man. You can practice with me because I'm no threat to you. You've heard me say that I am not husband material, which means I'll never again become involved in a serious relationship on any level. I might date later, casual outings, but that's it.

"Therefore, you are perfectly safe with me. You can learn to relax, chat, interact with me and know I won't take advantage of you, nor ask anything of you. Get it?''

"I think that's borderline crazy, Harrison."

"No, it's not. You're teaching me how to be a father. I'll teach you how to enjoy the company of men. Sounds like a fair trade to me.''

"Definitely crazy," Maggie said, getting to her feet. "I've got to go home.''

"Whoa," Harrison said, closing the distance between them. "We came in here in the first place to discuss something about tomorrow. Remember?''

"Oh. Yes," Maggie said, then cleared her throat. "Well, I don't work tomorrow because I'm off Friday and Sunday so I can do the story hour on Saturday. I thought maybe we could go get a Christmas tree with the kids right after school, then put it up and decorate it. It was just a thought. That is if you even use a fresh tree.''

''Sounds good, and yes, I like the smell of a real tree in the house, not an artificial one. I think that's a great idea. We'll start getting ready for the holiday season. This first one without Lisa is going to be very difficult for the kids, I imagine, so we might as well get it going and deal with the fallout.''

''Yes, that's what I was thinking, too.'' Maggie paused. ''Harrison, would you please back up a step or two? You're in my space, invading my comfort zone.''

Harrison glanced down at the floor, mentally measuring the distance between them, then frowned as he looked at Maggie again.

''Your zone is oversize,'' he said.

''Well, that's for me to say. It *is* my zone, you know.''

''I realize that,'' Harrison said, nodding, ''but you're learning how to be comfortable around men, around me, remember?''

''I never agreed to your plan to—''

''Check this out, Maggie,'' Harrison interrupted. ''If I was a man who was chatting with you and who also wished to kiss you—'' he placed his hands lightly on her shoulders ''—I'd need to be this close to you. If I backed up out of *your* comfort zone, I'd have to raise my voice to talk to you and the kiss would be impossible from that distance.''

''I—''

''But if I'm here, in what is really quite a normal comfort zone for the average person,'' Harrison went on, ''we can converse in normal tones and—'' he lowered his head and brushed his lips over Maggie's ''—things could progress further if they were meant to be.''

Oh, dear heaven, Maggie thought. Harrison's lips fluttering over hers had been as light as a butterfly's wings. But she could still feel his lips, the lingering faint taste of him, and...

His hands. They were there on her shoulders and the heat from them was suffusing her entire body. This was not a comfort zone, this was an erogenous zone and it was...wonderful. Absolutely marvelous and— No, darn it, it was terrifying and she wanted no part of this. Then again...

''Maggie?'' Harrison said, not removing his hands from her shoulders. ''Do you still want me to back up, get out of your zone?''

''No. Yes. I don't know. You're confusing me, Harrison.''

''That's good,'' he said. ''If you're confused, then it means that your beliefs aren't etched in stone and can't be budged. There's no reason in the world for you to sentence yourself to a life alone, Maggie Conrad. Me? After the kids are grown and gone, then yeah, I'll be alone, and nothing can change that. But that's not true for you. It just isn't.''

"You don't know me well enough to make such a statement, Harrison," Maggie said firmly.

"Don't I?"

Harrison moved his hands to frame Maggie's face, then lowered his head and captured her lips in a searing kiss. Maggie's hands flew up to splay on his chest with every intention of shoving him away, but the instant her palms felt the hard wall of muscle she gripped handfuls of his sweater and pulled him closer.

Harrison parted Maggie's lips and delved his tongue into the dark sweetness beyond, savoring the taste of her, drinking of it like a thirsty man.

A little whimper caught in Maggie's throat.

A groan rumbled in Harrison's chest.

He broke the kiss, slowly, reluctantly, then dropped his hands from Maggie's flushed cheeks and took a step backward.

"You," he said, then cleared his throat when he heard the gritty quality of his voice. "You are not meant to spend your life alone, magical Maggie. You are a very passionate, very desirable woman. I envy the man you fall in love with. He'd damn well better deserve who and what you are."

"Don't swear in the house," Maggie said, then drew a wobbly breath. "I have to go home. Now."

Harrison nodded. "Good night, Maggie."

She hurried across the room, grabbed her tote bag and coat and left the house before putting her coat on. Harrison shoved his hands into his pockets and stared at the door that had closed behind Maggie.

"Oh, yeah," he said, "I envy the man you fall in love with, Maggie. I truly do." He sighed. "Time to get to work, Parker. Matt Tynan is counting on you."

As Harrison trudged up the stairs, his thoughts once again focused on Maggie.

Well, he should feel a little better, he supposed. According to Maggie he *wasn't* doing anything specific to cause her to be so jittery around him. Her edginess was caused by the fact that he was simply a man. His glaring flaw was not at fault...this time.

One thing was for sure. Maggie sure hadn't been nervous when she'd returned his kiss in total abandon. She'd let herself go, given just as much as she was receiving. Imagine, just imagine, what it would be like to make love with Maggie Conrad, to have all of that passion, intensity, desire that was real and honest, directed at him, only for him. Just imagine...

"No don't," he said, as he entered the office and felt heat rocket throughout his body. "Not if you intend to get any work done in here."

Maggie, Maggie, he thought as he sat down and turned on the computer. He'd meant what he'd told her. As she taught him how to be a father that was worth a damn, he'd teach her how to relax and just be herself around men. Both lessons would have a tremendous influence on each of their individual happiness in the future.

It was just that…well, the thought of Maggie moving eagerly, willingly, into the arms of some faceless yahoo because she had conquered her ghosts and fears was not a picture he liked the looks of in his mind's eye.

Maggie was not worldly and wise, didn't know the rules of the singles' scene, how to tell the good guys from the ones who wanted nothing more than to hustle her into bed.

Maybe he wasn't doing Maggie any great favor by helping her overcome her skittishness around men. She might venture out into the unknown, as she apparently had once before, and be taken in by a sleazeball who would take full advantage of the innocence he saw and sensed in her.

But if Maggie didn't come out of her protective shell, she was destined to live her life alone, just as he would when the kids were grown and gone. Not good. Maggie had so much to offer, was sunshine itself on a cloudy day, would be a wonderful mother and a woman any sensible man would want to rush home to be with at the end of a work day.

He was doing the right thing by helping Maggie overcome her irrational fears. Just as she was doing the right thing by teaching him how to interact with his children in a proper manner. They were…yeah, they were friends, assisting the other in areas where they were in need. Fine.

"Get to work, Parker," Harrison said, typing on the computer keyboard. "Come on, Gideon, give me a clue. Where are you?"

Maggie blanked her mind and didn't think during the drive from Harrison's house to her little guest cottage. She didn't think as she entered her cozy haven, then drew water in the tub for a leisurely bath. She didn't think as she sank into the warm, soothing water, leaned her head against the tile wall and closed her eyes.

And then she thought.

About Harrison.

And the kiss they had shared.

She relived every sensual second of that kiss, tucking the memories away in a private treasure chest in her heart. She savored the remembrance of the taste and unique male aroma of Harrison, of how strong yet gentle he was, of the heated desire that had swirled and churned and pulsed deep within her. She rejoiced in how feminine she had felt, how very womanly, vibrant and alive.

But as the water began to cool, her mind shifted to a darker place that held niggling voices that taunted her with the knowledge of how foolish it had been, how very dangerous and very, very wrong to have allowed Harrison Parker to kiss her and to have responded to that kiss, holding nothing of herself back from him.

"Dumb," Maggie said, pulling the plug in the tub and stepping onto the mat.

She dried with a fluffy towel, then slipped a flannel nightie over her head before plunking down on the edge of her double bed.

"Really dumb," she said, shaking her head.

She was supposed to chalk up that kiss as a lesson in how to be comfortable around men? Treat it like a homework assignment? Go with Harrison's asinine program that he would help her overcome her flaw while she was helping him learn how to be a devoted father?

Harrison was convinced that he was not husband material, could never love a woman the way he should, would never be able to do that. Therefore he had no intention of ever again engaging in a serious relationship with a woman.

Was that a bunch of baloney? A con? A sneaky way to break down her protective walls and eventually entice her into his bed?

No. She believed Harrison when he said his flaw could not be overcome. She didn't agree with him, but she knew that he believed it to be true.

His other flaw, his history of not performing well as a father, was correctable with her assistance, said Mr. Parker. Her flaw was definitely fixable and he fully intended to help her do just that as a payback for what she was doing for him.

There was nothing sinister about it.

It was just the strangest situation she'd ever been in. And the most dangerous, and exciting, terrifying, and wondrous, scary, and ecstasy in its purest form.

"Confusing," Maggie said, nodding decisively. "Most definitely confusing."

She got to her feet, deciding that any person who was a befuddled mess to the degree that she was needed a huge dish of ice cream smothered in chocolate sauce to soothe her jangled nerves.

And while she ate her sinful treat she would not think.

A light snow started to fall the next afternoon when the Parker family and Maggie stood in a Christmas tree lot and scrutinized the offerings.

"Oh, this is perfect," Maggie said, smiling. "It's snowing while we pick out a tree. Doesn't that put you in the Christmas spirit, kids?"

"We have to go home now," David said. "My mom never let us be outside when it was snowing because we'd get all wet and catch colds. We have to go. Right now."

"No, David," Harrison said, "we don't. You're all wearing warm jackets, mittens, hats. We're not going to be out here that long and we're not leaving until we find a tree we all like."

"But Mom—"

"I'm your dad," Harrison said, "and I make the rules now."

"Well, if I get sick and die it will be all your fault," David said, glaring at his father.

"Fair enough," Harrison said, then tilted his head back and opened his mouth.

"What are you doing?" David said.

"Tasting a snowflake," Harrison said.

"No way," David said. "That's bad. Mom said there's germs in snow because there's gunk in the air and ozone or something."

"Delicious," Maggie said, catching a snowflake on the tip of her tongue. "One snowflake isn't that gunky, David. It's sugar and spice."

"I want some sugar and stuff," Benny said, sticking out his tongue.

"Me, too," Chelsey said, doing the same.

"What kind of father are you?" David yelled at Harrison. "Your children are swallowing gunky germs."

"I'm a father who is having fun with his kids," Harrison said, "except for the one who is hollering his head off."

"Yeah, right," David said, folding his arms over his chest. "Like you're really into having fun with your kids. Wrong."

"We're all having fun, David," Maggie said quickly, as she saw the flicker of pain cross Harrison's face at David's biting words. "One snowflake. Try it. You won't die of germs, I promise."

"I got mine," Benny said, jumping up and down.

"Me, too," Chelsey said. "Come on, David, don't be such a crabby apple."

"I'm not sticking my tongue out like a dork," David said. "I— Hey, one landed on my nose." He pushed the snowflake into his mouth with one finger.

"There. I did it. Okay? Is everyone off my case now?"

"Oh, my gosh, you're turning green, David," Harrison said. "Now you're blue, purple. The gunky germs are getting you, kid. You're doomed."

David laughed. "Cut it out, Dad. I mean, jeez, people are going to think we're all nuts."

"No, David," Harrison said, giving him a light punch on the arm, "they're just going to think we're having a lot of fun. Now then, let's get serious about picking out this tree."

"These are too small," David said, starting off with Chelsey and Benny right behind him. "We need a six-footer at least."

Harrison and Maggie exchanged a warm smile, then followed the children.

"Nicely done," Maggie said. "You defused David before he ruined the outing. I'm impressed."

"Really?" Harrison said, appearing extremely pleased with himself.

"Really," Maggie said.

Harrison frowned in the next instant. "Lisa sure had some strange ideas that I didn't even know about. Kids can't play in the snow? Or catch a snowflake on their tongue? Or have hamburgers for dinner?" He sighed. "I have a feeling there are a lot more things about Lisa that I don't have a clue about."

"Put that on hold for now," Maggie said. "Your trio is standing in front of a tree that has got to be at least ten feet tall."

"Oh, cripe," Harrison said, quickening his step.

Maggie followed at a slower pace, savoring the warm, fuzzy feeling of having just plain old, not-even-confusing-or-complicated fun.

Six

The seven-foot tree, which had been a compromise between a six-foot and a ten-foot one, sparkled with a rainbow of colored lights and a multitude of ornaments.

Harrison and David had worked together to get the tree secured in the stand, then they toted the necessary boxes down from the attic. Harrison had called and had a huge pizza delivered to keep up the energy of the decorators and Christmas carols played on the stereo.

Maggie took the lid off a shoe box she found at the bottom of a larger carton.

"Oh, look at these ornaments," she said, smiling. "They're all handmade." She lifted out a paper angel that had green hair and red wings and turned it over. "You made this when you were four years old, Chelsey. That's what it says on the back here. It's a marvelous angel. We have to find special places for all of these works of art you three did."

"They don't go on the tree," David said.

"Why not?" Maggie said.

"My mom said they were cute and stuff, but they wrecked how the tree looked because the rest of the ornaments were bought at the store and were expensive and...she said she would keep the ones we made in that box.''

"Harrison?'' Maggie said, frowning.

Harrison lifted one shoulder in a shrug. ''That's how Lisa did it. We all looked through the ornaments in that box every few years, but none of them were hung on the tree.''

"But these are so special,'' Maggie said. ''Don't you agree, Harrison? As a father, wouldn't you be proud to see these masterpieces hanging on the tree?'' She stared at him intensely as she held out the box to him.

"Oh. Right. You betcha,'' Harrison said, taking the box. ''New rule, guys. These ornaments all get places of honor on the tree.''

Chelsey giggled. ''We're going to hang my angel with green hair on the tree, Daddy?''

"Dumb,'' David said.

Harrison placed the angel on a limb, then picked up the next offering in the shoe box, flipping it over to read what was written on the back.

"Ladies and gentlemen,'' he boomed, ''we have here a purple reindeer with six legs made by the famous artist David Parker when he was three years old.''

"Oh, man,'' David said, rolling his eyes and laughing. ''That is so gross.''

"It's genius-level work, young man,'' Harrison said, slipping the yarn loop over the end of a branch.

"I made some. I made some," Benny said, jumping up and down. "Find one I made, Daddy."

"Okay," Harrison said. "Let's see. Yep, here we go. It says on the back that this was made by you when you were two years old." He laughed. "What is it, Benny?"

"It's a Christmas tree," Benny said, continuing his impersonation of a pogo stick.

"I knew that," Harrison said. "It's a Christmas tree with branches on one side only. A very unique Christmas tree, I must say."

"Benny had to use those dorky plastic scissors when he was a really little kid," David said. "They don't cut too good. He got tired of messing with that tree and just whacked off the branches on the other side. I remember. I saw him do it."

"It's a cool tree," Harrison said, slipping it onto a limb.

Laughter danced through the air as Harrison continued to announce the name and age of the creator of each of the homemade ornaments, then placed them on the tree.

Oh, look at them, Maggie thought, sweeping her gaze over Harrison and the children. What a beautiful scene this was, complete with the marvelous sound of laughter. She would remember this moment, cherish it as the treasure it was.

"That is one fine-looking tree," Harrison said finally. "All that's missing is the angel on top and we've got it whipped. Has anyone seen the angel?"

David snatched it from a box and held it against his chest with both hands.

"No," he said. "Mom always put the angel on the top of the tree. She said it was her job. No one else is going to do it."

"We can't have a tree with no angel on top, David," Chelsey said frowning, then stuck her thumb in her mouth.

"Give me the angel, David," Harrison said quietly, extending one hand. "It's going on the top of the tree where it belongs."

"No," David said, taking a step backward. "Mom can't do it so…" Tears filled his eyes. "No."

"David," Harrison said firmly, "give it to me."

"You don't even care that it was Mom's special job to put the angel on top of the tree," David yelled. "I bet you want it to be *your* special job now, but no way, Dad. Last year when we decorated the tree you weren't even home. You don't have the right to put this angel on the top and you're not going to."

Harrison's shoulders slumped. "David, I realize I wasn't here last year when you decorated the tree but I didn't know that your mother had picked that night to do it. I was working late in Washington and when I got home… Never mind. We'll just leave the angel off and—"

"No, we gotta have the angel on top," Chelsey said, her bottom lip starting to tremble.

Oh, dear heaven, Maggie thought, this beautiful evening was falling apart. She couldn't help but won-

der why Lisa hadn't told Harrison about the tree decorating plans the previous year so he could be certain
he'd be here, but the important thing now was to
solve this problem before the lovely memories created tonight were shattered. She could tell by the expression on Harrison's face and his body language
that he was at a loss as to what to do.

Think, Maggie, she ordered herself. Fix this situation. Fast.

"David," she said, "I realize from what you are
saying that it was a tradition for your mother to place
the angel on top of the tree, but she's no longer here.
That doesn't mean the tradition should be forgotten
any more than you've forgotten your mother. That
would be very wrong.

"I think," she went on, "that the tradition needs
to be passed on, not thrown away. I sincerely believe
that your mother would approve of *you* being the one
to tend to the angel now."

"Me?" David said, his eyes widening.

"Oh, yes," Maggie said. "Most definitely you."

"I thoroughly agree," Harrison said.

"Fine," Maggie said.

Harrison stepped closer to her.

"Thank you," he whispered in her ear. "I was on
very thin ice there."

"I can't do it," David said. "Mom would never
let me go up that ladder."

"I give you permission to climb the ladder, David," Harrison said. "I'll stand right behind you just

in case you slip, but I don't see that happening. What do you say? Will you put the angel on the top of the tree?''

"Please, David?" Chelsey said.

David looked at the angel, the top of the tree, then nodded.

"Okay," he said. "It's my special job now. Maggie, if anybody hassles me about it next year, you remind them that I'm supposed to do it until I grow up and live in my own house.''

Oh, David, Maggie thought. Didn't he realize that she wouldn't be here with all of them next year? Didn't he realize that what she was sharing with them was temporary? Didn't he realize that she wasn't a member of this family?

"Maggie?" David said. "Will you tell my dad, and Chelsey and Benny next year if they forget?''

"I…" Maggie said, aware of the achy sensation of threatening tears that gripped her throat. "Yes, David, I'll tell them, but they won't forget. The job is too special, too important. No one will forget that you're to place the angel on the top of the tree.''

"Good," David said decisively.

Harrison moved the ladder into place, then David made his way cautiously upward, the angel in one hand. He leaned toward the tree, causing Maggie to hold her breath, then slipped the angel in place on the very top.

Benny hopped up and down in approval, Chelsey clapped her hands, and Maggie drew a much needed breath when David was down from his perch and standing safely on the floor.

"Perfectly done, David," Harrison said. "I'm proud of you."

Maggie went around the room, snapping off the lights.

"What are you doing?" Chelsey said. "Do we have to go to bed now?"

"No, it's not that late," Maggie said. "When I was growing up we had traditions, too. When the tree was all decorated, we'd turn out the lights and see how beautiful our creation was. I'm sharing that tradition with all of you. Okay?"

"Cool," David said, then the last lamp went dark. "Wow. Look at that tree. It's awesome."

"We did a super job," Harrison said, "working as a team."

"Can we keep your tradition forever, Maggie?" Chelsey said. "Or do we have to give it back. I really like how the tree looks with all the lamps turned off."

"You can keep my tradition," Maggie said, smiling. "It's a gift from me to all of you."

"Cool," David repeated, his gaze riveted on the tree.

"Cool," Benny echoed.

The next CD clicked into place on the stereo and the lilting sound of "Silent Night" floated through the air. Before he even knew he was going to do it, Harrison began to sing along. Maggie joined him, then David shrugged and began to sing, prompting Chelsey and Benny to do the same.

She was a breath away from bursting into sentimental tears, Maggie thought. What was happening at that moment was so dear, so pure and real. It brought memories of wonderful Christmases with her parents flooding back to touch her heart. But it also flickered ahead to next Christmas when she would be alone once again, causing a chill to course through her.

No, Maggie, she admonished herself. Don't do that. Don't look at the future, just savor the now and the beauty of what is taking place. She would etch it indelibly in her mind, her heart, her very soul, so she could reach for it and relive it whenever her aloneness inched toward loneliness. She'd remember every detail, every member of the Parker family. She'd never forget them. Nor the kisses shared with Harrison.

The song ended and a peppy rendition of "Jingle Bells" was next. Harrison snapped on a lamp. Maggie sniffled.

"What's wrong?" he said, looking over at her.

"Nothing," she said, smiling. "It was just so beautiful. You know, singing 'Silent Night' in front of the gorgeous tree and…" She sniffled again. "Ignore me. It's a woman thing. A Kodak moment. A Hallmark card with living, breathing people."

"Ah," Harrison said, nodding.

"Who are the Hallmarks?" Chelsey said. "We're

all Parkers and we are the ones who did the tree stuff and sang the song and everything.''

''You're absolutely right, Chelsey,'' Harrison said.

''Well, close,'' Maggie said. ''I'm not a Parker, honey. I'm Maggie Conrad, remember?''

''You could be a Parker if you wanted to,'' Chelsey said. ''Do you? Want to?''

''Oh…well, um…'' Maggie said, feeling a warm flush stain her cheeks. ''My goodness, it's snack time. Who wants ice cream?''

''I do,'' Chelsey said.

''Two scoops,'' David said, heading toward the kitchen.

''Two scoops,'' Benny said, marching after his big brother.

The trio disappeared from view and Maggie snapped on the remaining lamps in the living room.

''Ice cream, Harrison?'' she said, not looking at him.

''What? Oh, sure, I'll have some.'' Harrison paused. ''It's amazing sometimes, isn't it? How innocent children are? How they view things as being just a matter of deciding that's how it could be? Do you want to be a Parker? Just say the word and it's a done deal.''

''Chelsey was just chattering,'' Maggie said. ''She has probably forgotten she said that because she's concentrating on ice cream now. I'd better get out in the kitchen before those two scoops grow in number.''

"Yeah, David will find the biggest spoon in the drawer to measure his scoops." Harrison paused and frowned. "You know, Chelsey wasn't so far off the mark. If a person decides they *don't* want to be a Parker anymore they can do that, too. No problem. Lisa had reached that point."

"Don't do this, Harrison," Maggie said, narrowing her eyes. "Do not, I repeat, do not spoil this evening with gloom and doom. Are you listening to me? Hearing me? You created beautiful memories tonight with your children. Savor them, cherish them, don't tarnish them."

"You're part of the memories of tonight," he said, looking directly at her.

"I just happen to have been here."

"No, it's more than that and you know it," he said. "Things were falling apart when David got upset about the angel. Do you think I'll forget what you did, the way you reached my son and made everything okay again, magical Maggie? Not in this lifetime. You are most definitely a part of the memories."

"I..."

Harrison closed the distance between them and brushed one thumb lightly over Maggie's lips.

"Thank you for tonight, Maggie."

"No, I thank you," she said. "I plan to keep the memories made here this evening safely tucked away in my heart. I'll never forget watching David put that angel on the top of the tree." Maggie shook her head.

"Oh, don't get me started. I'll do my Hallmark card sniffle thing again."

"We're not Hallmarks," Harrison said, smiling at her warmly. "We're Parkers."

"No, I'm—"

"Leave it like that. Okay? Decorating a Christmas tree, singing 'Silent Night' in the glow of the lights— that's what a family does together. For tonight just go with it. You were a part of all of this. You were a Parker."

Before Maggie could decide if she was capable of speaking, noise erupted from the kitchen.

"No fair, David," Chelsey yelled. "Your scoops are bigger than mine and Benny's."

"That's because I'm older and bigger than you two," David hollered. "It takes more to fill me up."

"Go settle the war," Maggie said. "I'll be there in a minute."

Harrison nodded and strode across the room.

"I'm coming in there, you guys," he called out. "I'd better see equal servings in those bowls when I arrive."

"Oops," David said.

Maggie tuned out the voices coming from the kitchen as she wrapped her hands around her elbows and stared at the Christmas tree as Chelsey's and Harrison's words echoed in her mind. And her heart.

You could be a Parker if you wanted to. Do you? Want to?

For tonight just go with it. You were a part of all

*of this. You were a Parker…you were a Parker…you
were a Parker.*

Tears misted Maggie's eyes and she lifted her chin.

"Okay," she said softly. "I'm a Parker. Just for
tonight. That's all. Just one special night."

She squared her shoulders, drew a wobbly breath,
then forced herself to focus on the ice cream waiting
for her in the kitchen.

The ice cream was consumed, Harrison and David
carried the empty decoration boxes back up to the
attic, then Maggie read *The Night Before Christmas*
three times, laughing and firmly refusing to go for
number four.

While Harrison was tucking the children in bed,
Maggie performed her usual chore of setting the table
for breakfast the next morning. The task completed,
Maggie waited for Harrison to appear in the kitchen
per his routine.

She finally shrugged and wandered back into the
living room to discover that Harrison had once again
turned off the lamps. He was standing in front of the
Christmas tree, his hands shoved into the pockets of
his slacks. Maggie went to where he stood and
looked up at him questioningly.

"What are you doing?" she said.

"I like the tradition you shared with us. The tree
looks really nice like this." Harrison paused. "It's as
though…I don't know, this will probably sound
corny, but it's as though there is no world beyond

the circle of rainbow colors created by the lights. See? You're standing inside the circle.''

Maggie glanced down at the floor.

"Yes, I am,'' she said "I'm in a rainbow waterfall. There. How's that for corny? I assume your kiddies are all tucked in?''

"Tucked in and sound asleep,'' Harrison said. "Even David went right out. It was a big evening for them all. But, madam, the junior members of this firm do not exist at the moment because they're outside the circle.''

"I see,'' Maggie said, laughing softly. "Well, I'm afraid I'm going to have to exit the circle and be on my way. Are you planning to bring the they-don't-exist kids to story hour at the library tomorrow?''

"Kids? What kids?'' Harrison said, turning to face her. "I swear, Maggie, you're a slow study in the rules of the world created by the rainbow lights. Let me repeat: There is nothing beyond this circle.''

"Got it,'' she said, smiling. "We're the only two people who are in this world you invented.''

"Exactly.'' Harrison took one step forward to close the distance between them and cradled Maggie's face in his hands. "Now you understand how this works.''

"I...''

"Do you have any idea how beautiful you are standing in the rainbow waterfall?''

"Oh, no, I...''

"Oh, yes," Harrison said, then his mouth melted over hers.

The blue lights were a summer sky, the amber ones the sun. The green were a lush carpet of sweet grass, the white ones stars sparkling in a dark, velvet heaven. The red lights were heat, desire burning, building, consuming them.

Maggie's hands floated upward to encircle Harrison's neck. He dropped his hands from her face and encircled her with his arms, nestling her to his aroused body.

The kiss went on and on in the world within the mystical circle.

Harrison broke the kiss to draw a ragged breath, then spoke close to Maggie's moist lips.

"I want you, Maggie," he said, his voice gritty. "It has nothing to do with me helping you be comfortable with men while you're teaching me how to be an adequate father. Nothing. This is me, just me, wanting to make love with you with an intensity like nothing I've experienced before."

"Oh, but—"

"I know, I know," he said. "I have nothing to offer you as that man, but I had to say it, tell you, how much I desire you, want you." He dropped his arms to his sides. "Step out of the circle, Maggie, out of this world. Go. Because if you stay..."

For tonight just go with it. You were a part of all of this. You were a Parker....a Parker...a Parker.

The words hummed in Maggie's mind as she met

Harrison's gaze, seeing the desire there that she knew mirrored what he could glimpse in her own eyes.

"I earned my place in this circle tonight," she said, hardly above a whisper. "I am a Parker, just for tonight. One stolen night, Harrison. I want to make love with you in this world, knowing it won't exist in the light of the new day."

"Ah, Maggie," Harrison said, pulling her into his arms and holding her tightly. "Are you sure? You'll have no regrets? Can you promise me you won't be sorry? I couldn't handle it if you were."

"I promise," she said. "But you must understand that it is meant to be only for this night. The night I was a Parker, but never again. We won't talk about what took place here, in this world, we'll just go on as we were before, with each of us doing what we choose with the memories of it. That's how it must be, Harrison. Can you do that? Promise me that?"

Harrison nodded slowly, but didn't speak. He kissed Maggie again, so gently, so reverently, as though she was made of the most delicate china, then raised his head and reached for the bottom of Maggie's oversize sweater. She stiffened and frowned.

"No?" Harrison said, looking directly into her eyes.

"I... It's just that it's been such a long time since I..." Maggie sighed. "And what if the children wake up and... I'm sorry. I'm acting very childish, very unsophisticated. I must really be impressing you with my worldliness."

Harrison smiled. "Your lack of war weary world-liness is one of the things that makes you so unique, so special." He paused. "One of the rules of existing within this rainbow circle is that we must be totally honest. Oh, and the kids are down for the count, thoroughly exhausted. Okay? Maggie, why do you wear such huge clothes?"

"*Totally* honest?"

"Yes."

"Well, okay, I guess. The clothes I wear make me feel sort of invisible, I think. It's safe in here beneath the bulky sweaters and sweatshirts. Does that make sense?"

Harrison nodded. "But you're safe with *me* so you don't need that enormous sweater."

"I..." Maggie started, then stopped and lifted her chin. "You're right."

"You're sure?"

"Yes." Maggie stepped back, pulled the sweater over her head then dropped it on the floor.

Harrison's breath caught. Maggie wasn't wearing a bra, a fact that was not discernible because of the size of the sweater. Her breasts were lush, full, and her waist was tiny above the baggy slacks.

"You're staring at me," Maggie said, struggling against the urge to snatch the sweater from the floor and cover her breasts.

"I can't help it. You're exquisite." Harrison reached out one hand toward Maggie's breasts, then stopped. "This isn't fair to you. We're equal partners in this momentous decision we've made for tonight."

With no wasted motions Harrison removed his sweater, shoes and socks, jeans and briefs, then lowered his arms to his sides.

"Oh, Harrison," Maggie said, awe ringing in her voice as she swept her gaze over him. "*You* are exquisite. So perfectly proportioned, one part of you flowing into the next like a sculpture."

"Equal partners," he said, his voice gritty with growing passion.

"Yes."

Maggie removed the remainder of her clothes, her trepidation gone, her desire and anticipation of what was to come causing her heart to race and cheeks to flush.

Harrison gazed at her, marveling at the womanly slope of her hips, the long, satiny length of her legs. Beneath those baggy clothes Maggie had hidden the epitome of femininity. She was beautiful.

"So beautiful," he said. "I feel so honored that you're allowing me to see, touch, what you've kept hidden. It's a gift from you to me and I'll cherish it always."

Harrison closed the distance between them and pulled Maggie into his arms. She went willingly, welcoming his mouth as it captured hers. Their desire heightened and without breaking the kiss they sank to the carpet, holding fast to each other.

When Harrison broke the kiss they stretched out,

a body soft and curved nestled against a body hard and nicely muscled. They kissed, tasted, savored. They touched with fingers eager to explore, discover the mysteries of the other, then lips followed the heated path where hands had gone.

The rainbow waterfall cascaded over them, creating shifting colors on their moist skin. Desire hummed, and churned, and burned within them.

Harrison drew the sweet flesh of one of Maggie's breasts into his mouth, laving the nipple with his tongue. A soft sigh of womanly pleasure whispered from Maggie's throat. He paid homage to her other breast, as her fingertips skittered over the curls of crisp hair on his chest.

The heat within them was a brush fire out of control, raging, consuming them with want and need like nothing they had known before.

"Harrison," Maggie said finally, her voice trembling. "Please. I...I feel so... I want you so much. Please."

"Yes. I want you, too, more than I can even begin to tell you. I... Maggie, I need to protect you, but I don't have anything to—"

"Shh," she said, brushing her lips over his. "It's all right. I'm on the pill because my system was out of sync and the pill helped to—"

"Good," Harrison interrupted. "That's very good, because I don't know what I would do if I had to stop right now."

"Please, Harrison, make love to me."

He moved over her and into her, watching her face for any sign that he was hurting her, but seeing only pleasure in its purest form. He filled her, sighing from deep in his chest at the ecstasy of it, of meshing with Maggie, of being one with her. He looked directly into her eyes that were a smoky hue of desire and began the rhythm that had belonged to lovers since the beginning of time, but was theirs alone in the circle of rainbow lights.

He increased the tempo and Maggie clung to his shoulders, matching him beat for beat, raising her hips to bring him deeper yet within her, as they were lifted up and away toward the top of the waterfall. They burst upon it moments apart, whispering the name of the other, then tumbled down in a swirl of sensations so intense they stole the very breath from their bodies.

Harrison collapsed against Maggie, sated, spent, awed. He gathered his last ounce of strength and moved off of her, wrapping his arm around her waist as she nestled her head on his shoulder.

Bodies cooled. Hearts returned to normal beats. Breathing slowed. And memories of what they had just shared were tucked away in private chambers within them.

Minutes passed and neither spoke, each reliving every kiss, every caress, every discovery, with awe and wonder.

"Unbelievable," Harrison finally said.

"Yes," Maggie said quietly. "I never knew it

could be like that. So…so… I don't have the words to describe it.''

''I don't, either,'' Harrison said, sifting his fingers through her silky hair. ''It's as though… This will sound weird, but it's as though it was the first time for me. It was new, fantastic, like nothing I've ever had. It was ours, magical Maggie. I guess that's the best way to put it. It was ours.''

''On this stolen night. One stolen night when I was a Parker. Here, in the rainbow circle that created our world where no one could be but us.''

''Yes.'' Harrison rested his lips lightly on Maggie's forehead.

''I could fall asleep so easily,'' Maggie said. ''I've got to go home, Harrison.''

''Not yet.''

Maggie laughed softly. ''Do you want to explain to your children when they wake up in the morning why we're asleep by the Christmas tree as naked as the day we were born?''

''No,'' Harrison said, chuckling. ''That is not a scenario that thrills me.''

''And so I'll go home, but thank you for this night, Harrison,'' Maggie said. ''I mean that.''

''And I thank you. We gave, we received, we shared, holding nothing back. It was so honest, real, special, very special.''

''Yes, it was.''

Maggie moved out of Harrison's embrace, knowing she didn't want to go, to break the spell, to leave the world within the circle of rainbow lights. She reached for her clothes and with a sigh, Harrison sat up and sought his own.

"I don't want this night to end," he said, rolling to his feet. "There. How's that for honest?"

"Ditto, ditto, ditto," Maggie said, then rose and finished dressing.

"I'll see you at story hour at the library tomorrow," she said, as she slipped on her shoes.

"Yeah, okay."

"I— Dear heaven," Maggie said, as a scream reverberated through the air from upstairs.

"Benny," Harrison said, starting toward the stairs. "He has nightmares sometimes about Lisa."

"Mommy!" Benny yelled. "Mommy!"

Harrison ran up the stairs with Maggie right behind him. They hurried down the hall and into Benny's room, Harrison snapping on the lamp on the nightstand. Benny was sitting up in bed, his little face pale and streaked with tears, his hair damp. A shudder swept through him.

"I'm here, buddy," Harrison said, sitting down on the edge of the bed. "You had a bad dream, that's all."

"Mommy was...Mommy was..." Benny said, a sob catching in his throat.

"Do you want me to lay with you for a while, Benny?" Harrison said.

"No," Benny said, pushing at Harrison's chest with both hands. "No. Mommy said you didn't want to be with us. She said you'd rather work and be away instead of here. She said that. Lots of times. She did. I don't want you to lay on my bed, Daddy. I want…I want Maggie.''

"Benny," Maggie said, coming closer. "I have to go home now. Your daddy will stay right here with you until you go back to sleep. He won't leave you."

"He might 'cause my mommy said he doesn't keep promises good."

A flash of anger directed at Lisa Parker rushed through Maggie and she drew a steadying breath before she attempted to speak again.

"If your father made me a promise, Benny," she said finally, "I would trust him to keep it. I would. If he promises to lay with you until you're asleep, he will. I know he will, Benny bug."

"No," Benny said, fresh tears spilling onto his cheeks.

Harrison got to his feet.

"All right, Benny," he said, his voice ringing with raw pain. "I understand." He shifted his gaze to Maggie and her breath caught as she saw the anguish in his eyes, on his face. "Will you lay with him just until he calms down and goes back to sleep?"

"Yes, of course," she said, "but… No, this isn't the time to discuss it but…"

Harrison frowned. "Discuss what?"

"We'll talk about it later," Maggie said, then looked at Benny. "May I share your pillow for a bit, Benny bug?"

Benny lifted his arms toward Maggie and Harrison turned and strode from the room. Back downstairs he stared at the Christmas tree, then flipped the switch on the wall to turn off the rainbow of lights.

"Reality check, Harrison," he said, with a weary, defeated sigh. "Your kids hate you. Your wife hated you. You're a big-time winner, one swell guy." He shook his head. "Hell."

He snapped on a lamp and slouched onto the sofa, feeling as though his very thoughts were crushing him into dust.

God, he thought, Lisa had actually told his children that he'd rather work than be with them? That he didn't keep his promises? He'd wanted to be with his kids, but it seemed like Lisa had started acting like a guard around them, not letting him get close to them, closed the ranks and left him on the outside looking in.

He couldn't remember breaking one promise he'd made to those children. Last year when he hadn't been there to decorate the tree had Lisa told them he'd promised to come home, but had broken that promise? She hadn't even informed him that the night had been chosen to do the tree as a family.

Had Lisa hated him so much that she'd set about poisoning his children's minds against him? Would Lisa have actually done that? Hell, he didn't know. As time had passed he'd had to face the fact that he really didn't know his wife at all. He'd worked longer and longer hours rather than come home to a stranger who more often than not was angry at him for his most recent sin that she'd decided he'd committed.

What could he have done differently to keep alive the love that Lisa and he had once had? He didn't have a clue. She'd stopped loving him. He'd stopped loving her. And even if he'd been given a chance, he wouldn't have known how to fix it.

Harrison shifted his haunted gaze to the place by the tree where he and Maggie had made love.

Magical Maggie. He was going to savor the memories of this night, the lovemaking shared with Maggie Conrad. He was going to take those memories and use them to shove some of the ugly ones out of his mind and heart and take front row center.

"Damn straight," Harrison said. "Tonight was ours, mine and Maggie's and I'm keeping it."

A half hour later Harrison struggled to his feet and plodded back up the stairs to check on Maggie and Benny.

In Benny's room, Harrison stood next to the bed and allowed the warmth of the scene before him to chase away the last of the chill that had consumed him.

Maggie had removed her shoes and was sound asleep under the blankets on the bed. Benny was sleeping peacefully, his head on her shoulder, one little hand gripping her sweater. Their heads were touching on the pillow and their breathing was even and steady.

"You're safe now, Benny," Harrison said. "Right there in Maggie's arms, you're safe. I promise."

Seven

"Maggie! Maggie! Maggie!" Benny yelled. "You sleeped in my bed with me all night long."

Maggie shot bolt upright as she was jolted from a deep sleep and blinked several times, having absolutely no idea where she was. As the fog lifted, she looked at Benny and managed to produce a weak smile.

"Well, yes, I guess I did," she said, then yawned. "You have a very comfy bed, Benny bug. I bet I snored like a fuzzy bear."

Benny giggled, then slid from the bed, taking off at a run the moment his feet hit the floor.

"Maggie sleeped in my bed all night long," he hollered, as he dashed out the bedroom door to deliver his news to the rest of the family.

Within a few minutes a rumpled David and Chelsey were standing next to the bed, while Benny hopped up and down in excitement.

"How come you sleeped here?" Chelsey said. "How come you picked Benny's bed instead of mine?"

"I didn't intend to sleep over," Maggie said. "Benny had a bad dream and I agreed to lie with him until he fell back to sleep. And here I am, just like Goldilocks, having slept in baby bear's bed.'' She glanced at her watch. "I've got to get moving. I have to go home, shower and change and hustle to the library.''

"Is this where the party is?" Harrison said, coming into the room.

Great, Maggie thought dryly. Harrison was obviously showered and shaved, was wearing jeans and a black and white sweater, hair neatly combed, the whole nine yards. Not fair, considering she must look like a bag lady waking up on a park bench. Oh, yes, there he was—gorgeous Harrison Parker.

Images of the lovemaking shared with Harrison the previous night in the private circle of rainbow lights flashed in Maggie's mental vision and a warm flush stained her cheeks.

It had been so incredibly beautiful, so special…theirs, she mused dreamily. This was the morning after and she didn't regret what had taken place one iota. The memories were hers to keep and she intended to do exactly that. It had been just one stolen night. Just one. So be it. But she'd never forget it, would cherish it always.

"How are you this morning, Maggie?" Harrison said, looking at her intently.

"Perfect," she said, smiling at him warmly. "Everything is just fine.''

"Good," he said, matching her smile. "I feel rather perfect myself.''

They continued to gaze into each other's eyes, and her heart quickened. They'd agreed that what had transpired between them last night would not be discussed, yet Harrison obviously could not disguise the renewed desire that radiated from his eyes. Exquisite, sensual remembrances tumbled through her mind, one into the next.

"Yeah, well, um…" Harrison said finally, shifting his attention to the kids. "Who is ready for breakfast?"

"Are you gonna eat breakfast with us, Maggie?" Benny said.

"I'll just have a cup of coffee," she said, "then I'll be on my way. I am so grungy from sleeping in my clothes. One quick cup, then off I go to my little cottage to freshen up and be ready to see you later for story hour."

"'kay," Benny said.

"You guys go ahead and start on some cereal," Harrison said. "I need to talk to Maggie for a minute."

The trio ran from the room and Harrison sat down on the end of the bed. Maggie brushed away the blankets, pulled her knees up and wrapped her arms around them.

"Am I just knocking you over with how lovely I look in the morning?" she said, laughing. "Oh, this is really mortifying. I don't know who was more surprised to discover I was here, me or Benny."

Harrison turned his head to look at her. "It makes sense, you know."

"What does?"

"Think about it, Maggie. What if you'd already gone home when Benny had that nightmare? He didn't want any part of me, would probably have been upset for hours because he wouldn't allow me to comfort him. If you stayed here, lived here while you're being the nanny, per se, all the bases would be covered."

"Benny would have let you ease his fears if I hadn't been here," Maggie said.

"I don't believe that," Harrison said, his jaw tightening. "You heard what he said."

"Yes, I did. Harrison, this is none of my business, but it's beginning to sound like Lisa was determined that those children would be angry with you, wouldn't trust you or... It makes me so furious to think she— No, erase that. I'm overstepping."

"No, you're not," he said, then sighed wearily. "I'm putting the puzzle together and getting the same picture, too. Lisa lied to the kids about me, Maggie. She didn't tell me she planned to decorate the tree on a given night last year, then apparently told them I just couldn't be bothered to show up. She made it clear to them that I didn't keep my promises or..." He shook his head.

"I'm so sorry, Harrison," Maggie said quietly. "It's going to make things that much more difficult as you rebuild the bond with your children. Time.

That's what it's going to take. Time, with promises kept.''

"Yeah.'' Harrison paused. "Let's back up. Would you even consider living here temporarily? I still have to solve the problem of what to do with the kids when Christmas vacation starts. They have school next week, then they're off until after the new year.

"But I'm getting off the track again. I can't handle the idea that Benny might have another nightmare and just cry and cry because he doesn't want me to hold or hug him, Maggie. He fell asleep clutching your sweater, making certain you were there.''

Harrison stared up at the ceiling for a long moment to attempt to regain control of his emotions.

"It just breaks my heart to see him so scared,'' he said, his voice gritty, "knowing I'm helpless, that I can't... When the kids were babies I was the one who got up with them in the night because Lisa said she was too tired from tending to them all day. I liked doing it, I really did. It was special, private time with the one who was a baby then. I'd talk when I fed them the bottle, tell them about the adventures they'd have as they were growing up, about all the wonderful things yet to come and... Never mind.''

"You're a devoted, loving father, Harrison,'' Maggie said. "I don't know what happened between you and Lisa but somewhere along the line she...well, she poisoned their minds about you. That might not be a nice thing to say, but it's the way I see it.''

Harrison nodded. "She changed. About a year before she was killed she...I don't know... She was angry at me all the time it seemed, but refused to talk about it, tell me what was wrong. She built a wall around her and the kids and I couldn't reach any of them.

"I'd offer to play with them, and they'd say no. I always helped David with his homework but he suddenly didn't want me to. We'd go grocery shopping as a family on Saturday, but Lisa started doing it with the kids on Friday afternoon before I got home.

"I was so..." Harrison dragged both hands down his face. "I was so damn lonely in my own home. So I started working long hours, very long hours. I just didn't have anything to come home to. Oh, God, I wish I knew what I did to make Lisa hate me so much. She didn't just stop loving me, she actually came to hate me."

"Why are you assuming it was your fault?" Maggie said.

Harrison snapped his head around to look at her. "I was the one who was supposed to make her happy and I failed. I failed at being a husband, at...loving her, Maggie. Lisa wasn't happy and it was my job— for the lack of a better word—to be certain that she was."

"Oh, Harrison, that's not true," Maggie said. "If a person isn't content, at peace, happy within themselves, no one else can do it for them. You don't get married so someone will take over the responsibility of seeing to your happiness.

"Having a soul mate, a partner in life, is frosting on a cake that a person has already baked on their own. Your happiness is enhanced, is bigger and brighter, but it has to be there in the first place so it can be nurtured by that union."

Harrison frowned as he looked at Maggie intently.

"That's heavy stuff," he said.

"It's what I believe." Maggie took a deep breath and let it out slowly. "All right, Harrison, I'll stay here while I'm doing the Mary Poppins nanny thing. I can't bear the thought of Benny being alone and terrified from his nightmares either. But we're going to work on undoing the damage that Lisa did. We are.

"As for the Christmas break from school? I have vacation time saved up at the library and I'll take it then. You do understand, Harrison, that I'm assuming you're working diligently on that special project you told me about."

"I am, but it's slow going," he said. "You'll really do it? Stay here?"

"Yes."

"Ah, thank you, Maggie. I—"

"Daddy," Chelsey said, running into the room, "Benny dropped the jug of orange juice and it's all over the floor and the table and Benny and the cereal and the—"

"Okay, okay, Miss Seven O'clock News, I'm coming," Harrison said, getting to his feet.

Harrison and Chelsey hurried from the room with

An Important Message from the Editors

Dear Reader,

Because you've chosen to read one of our fine romance novels, we'd like to say "thank you!" And, as a **special** way to thank you, we've selected <u>two more</u> of the books you love so well **plus** an exciting Mystery Gift to send you — absolutely <u>FREE</u>!

Please enjoy them with our compliments...

Pam Powers

Lift here

How to validate your Editor's "Thank You" FREE GIFT

1. Peel off gift seal from front cover. Place it in space provided at right. This automatically entitles you to receive 2 FREE BOOKS and a fabulous mystery gift.

2. Send back this card and you'll get 2 brand-new *Romance* novels. These books have a cover price of $5.99 or more each in the U.S. and $6.99 or more each in Canada, but they are yours to keep absolutely free.

3. There's no catch. You're under no obligation to buy anything. We charge nothing—ZERO—for your first shipment. And you don't have to make any minimum number of purchases—not even one!

4. The fact is, thousands of readers enjoy receiving their books by mail from The Reader Service. They enjoy the convenience of home delivery...they like getting the best new novels at discount prices BEFORE they're available in stores... and they love their Heart to Heart subscriber newsletter featuring author news, horoscopes, recipes, book reviews and much more!

5. We hope that after receiving your free books you'll want to remain a subscriber. But the choice is yours— to continue or cancel, any time at all! So why not take us up on our invitation, with no risk of any kind. You'll be glad you did!

GET A *Free* MYSTERY GIFT...

SURPRISE MYSTERY GIFT COULD BE YOURS **FREE** AS A SPECIAL "THANK YOU" FROM THE EDITORS

The Editor's "Thank You" Free Gifts Include:

- *Two BRAND-NEW Romance novels!*
- *An exciting mystery gift!*

Yes!
I have placed my Editor's "Thank You" seal in the space provided above. Please send me 2 free books and a fabulous mystery gift. I understand I am under no obligation to purchase any books, as explained on the back and on the opposite page.

**PLACE
FREE GIFT
SEAL
HERE**

393 MDL DVFG   193 MDL DVFF

FIRST NAME	LAST NAME

ADDRESS

APT.#	CITY

STATE/PROV.   ZIP/POSTAL CODE

(PR-R-04)

Thank You!

The Reader Service — Here's How It Works:

Accepting your 2 free books and gift places you under no obligation to buy anything. You may keep the books and gift and return the shipping statement marked "cancel." If you do not cancel, about a month later we'll send you 3 additional books and bill you just $4.74 each in the U.S., or $5.24 each in Canada, plus 25¢ shipping & handling per book and applicable taxes if any.* That's the complete price and — compared to cover prices starting from $5.99 each in the U.S. and $6.99 each in Canada — it's quite a bargain! You may cancel at any time, but if you choose to continue, every month we'll send you 3 more books, which you may either purchase at the discount price or return to us and cancel your subscription.

*Terms and prices subject to change without notice. Sales tax applicable in N.Y. Canadian residents will be charged applicable provincial taxes and GST.

If offer card is missing write to: The Reader Service, 3010 Walden Ave., P.O. Box 1867, Buffalo, NY 14240-1867

BUSINESS REPLY MAIL
FIRST-CLASS MAIL   PERMIT NO. 717-003   BUFFALO, NY

POSTAGE WILL BE PAID BY ADDRESSEE

THE READER SERVICE
3010 WALDEN AVE
PO BOX 1341
BUFFALO NY 14240-8571

NO POSTAGE
NECESSARY
IF MAILED
IN THE
UNITED STATES

Chelsey continuing to announce further targets of the orange juice and Harrison telling her that orange had never been one of his favorite colors.

"Oh, Maggie Conrad," she said aloud, resting her chin on the top of her tented knees, "what have you done?"

She'd agreed to live under the same roof with Harrison Parker, that's what. Well, there were also three little chaperons in residence, too. But short people went to bed early and events like what had taken place last night took place in private, adult time.

But not again.

No, the agreement was made. It had been one night and one night only that was not to be discussed in the light of the new day that was now officially here. Fine. Now if she could just figure out a way to turn off the sensual images flitting in her mind's eye, she'd be in good shape.

Maggie glanced at her watch, then left the bed.

"Late to work. I'm going to be late to work for the first time in my life," she muttered, stomping from the room. "Maggie Conrad, you are out of control."

Harrison brought the children to the library for story hour, then once again set out to Christmas shop, determined to find some gifts for the kids.

He bought Benny a soft, huggable Velveteen Rabbit and the matching book about the rabbit who became real because he was loved. He selected a princess outfit for Chelsey, complete with a sparkling pink dress, a crown with plastic jewels and a wand with a glittering star on top. For David he chose an enormous 3-D floor puzzle of a dinosaur that would measure six-feet-square when it was completed.

Would the kids like what he'd picked out for them? Harrison wondered. He didn't know, he really didn't. All he could do was wait, hope and pray that their faces would light up with smiles when they opened their presents on Christmas morning. He wanted that to happen so damn much.

Harrison glanced at his watch and realized it was nearly time to return to the library to pick up the kids. He hid the shopping bags beneath a blanket at the far end of the SUV and drove through the heavy traffic.

He still needed to get a gift for Maggie, he mused. Didn't he? Well, sure, he did. She would be there on Christmas morning and he certainly didn't want her to feel left out with nothing to open. But maybe she'd feel uncomfortable if he gave her something, especially if her budget hadn't stretched far enough to buy gifts for the whole Parker clan.

Perhaps it would be best to take the kids shopping and have each one select something special for Maggie, some little thing like a scented candle or a pretty bar of soap. That shouldn't upset her if she had nothing to give in return.

But…well, *he* wanted to give Maggie a Christmas gift. Why it was suddenly so important to him he didn't know. It went beyond how grateful he was for everything she was doing for him, for his family. He just wanted her to know that he thought she was very special, very rare and wonderful.

Harrison pulled into a parking space by the library, turned off the ignition, then stared into space.

Very special, very rare and wonderful, he mentally repeated. Those were not lightweight emotions he was registering in regard to Maggie Conrad. Well, since he was totally confusing himself as to where those feelings were coming from and exactly what they meant, he'd put them on a back burner and go get his kids.

"Talked to any other ostriches lately, Parker?" he muttered, getting out of the vehicle.

There were twice as many kids in the children's room of the library than there had been the week before, and the end of the designated hour was a loud gathering of arriving parents and chattering kids. A mother was having a conversation with Maggie as Harrison rounded up his brood, and he told them to just wave goodbye to her because she was busy.

"I want to give her a hug," Benny said.

"You can hug her tonight at the house," Harrison said, urging the trio forward. "Go."

"No," Benny said, "I want to give Maggie a hug *now*."

"Save this hug and add one to it at the house," Harrison said. "Then you can hug her twice."

"Oh," Benny said, nodding. "'kay."

Son of a gun, Harrison thought. He'd nipped that

tantrum-waiting-to-happen in the bud. Score one for Dad.

During the drive home Harrison explained that Maggie would be a little later than usual arriving to make dinner because she needed to go to her house first to pack a suitcase.

"Why?" Chelsey said, her eyes widening. "Maggie isn't going away, is she? With her suitcase? Daddy?"

"No, no," Harrison said quickly. "She's going to be staying with us, sleeping at our house at night for a while. She's also going to use her vacation time to take care of you during Christmas break from school so I can work during the day."

"Cool," David said.

"Cool," Benny echoed.

"Is she going to sleep in Benny's bed again?" Chelsey said. "Don't I get a turn having her sleep with me?"

"Maggie will have her own room down the hall from you," Harrison said. "There's still an extra bedroom upstairs, you know, even though I made one of them into an office."

"Oh," Chelsey said. "How long is 'a while'? You said Maggie would sleep at our house for a while."

"I'm not certain," Harrison said, frowning. "At least until you go back to school after the holiday break. It depends a lot on the special project I'm working on when you go to bed."

"You work in your office after we're asleep?" David said.

"Yes," Harrison said. "I spend the day on assignments I've contracted for and the extra hours at night on an important project I need to complete as quickly as possible."

"Yeah, but if we're sleeping and you're working," David said, "who's going to talk to Maggie? Don't you think she'll get lonely just sitting in the living room all by herself?"

Lonely in his own home, Harrison thought. He'd been down that chilling road and it was a living nightmare. But that scenario didn't apply to Maggie.

"No, she won't get lonely," he said. "You have to remember that Maggie lives alone now. She's used to filling her evening hours without anyone to talk to."

"Maybe I should stay up later and keep her company," David said.

Harrison chuckled. "Nice try, buddy, but no cigar."

"Maybe Maggie will do her tradition when she's by herself," Chelsey said. "You know, turn off the lamps and look at the Christmas tree. That would be nice."

Oh, thanks a bunch, Chelsey, Harrison thought dryly. That statement had just slam-dunked him with instant images of that private circle of colors, the rainbow waterfall where only he and Maggie were allowed to exist, where they'd made love so exquisitely beautiful that it was—

Heat rocketed through Harrison's body and he shifted a bit on the seat.

Don't go there, Parker, he ordered himself. Just don't do it.

"So!" he said, a tad too loudly. "What was Maggie's story about today? Benny, you go first."

The kids chattered the rest of the way to the house, but as Harrison pulled into the driveway he realized he didn't have a clue as to what Maggie's story had been.

He'd spent the time mentally pushing away the sensual images in his mind of making love with Maggie Conrad in the mystical circle of rainbow lights. Images that kept creeping back with a tenacity that was exhausting to struggle against.

At the house David made a beeline for the television with Benny on his heels. Chelsey brought an armload of dolls from her room and settled onto the floor with the announcement that they all needed their hair brushed.

Harrison collected sheets, pillow, blankets, bedspread and a stack of towels and washcloths from the linen closet upstairs and made up the bare twin bed in the spare room. He set the towels on the dresser and glanced around.

Not great, but not horrible, he supposed. It was a small room, but there was a slipper rocker that Maggie might like to sit in and read or whatever, and a desk against one wall. It was just…a room.

But he knew, just somehow knew, that once magical Maggie took up residency within these four walls there would be a welcoming warmth here that hadn't existed before. Maggie did that. Wherever she went, she brought sunshine with her.

Harrison sat down on the edge of the bed, then got to his feet in the next instant and smoothed the spread.

Stay away from Maggie's bed, he told himself. He was having enough trouble looking at the Christmas tree and dealing with the memories that came flooding over him each time he glanced at it, without envisioning Maggie sleeping in this very bed. Just down the hall from him. In the quiet of the night. When private worlds could be created and—

"I'm outta here," Harrison said, striding from the room.

Eight

Late at night a week later, Harrison stared at the computer screen in his office, narrowed his eyes and nodded.

Okay, he thought. Okay. He was *finally* making some progress on the project for Matt Tynan.

Harrison rotated his neck in an attempt to loosen the tight muscles that were beginning to give him a doozy of a headache. He leaned back in his chair, rested his head on the top and stared at the ceiling.

After hours and hours of work, he mused, he had found three top-secret files he had been unable to hack into, could not, so far, decipher the codes necessary to gain entry to examine the information. He had all his eggs in those three baskets, hoping that one of the files contained the data that Matt desperately needed about Gideon.

If he was wrong, if none of the three hit pay dirt, then he was baffled as to where else to look. He would have failed.

"So what else is new?" he said, dragging his hands down his face. "I'm an expert at failing."

He lifted his head and looked at the empty corner of his desk where a framed picture of a smiling Lisa had been until he'd put it on the closet shelf several nights before. The photograph had been taken on a beach in Florida the year they'd taken David and a toddling Chelsey to Disney World.

That was a long time ago, Harrison thought, still staring at the vacant corner of the desk. Back when Lisa had been happy. It had been a great trip with lots of smiles and laughter, a young family having fantastic adventures on their vacation.

Back when Lisa was happy.

Harrison sighed and tore his gaze from the edge of the desk to rest his head once again on the top of the chair.

According to Maggie's philosophy, he thought, Lisa had been responsible for her own happiness. Whatever further joy he brought into her life would be frosting on her cake, or some such thing.

Was that really true? Had he been scrambling to frost a cake that no longer existed because Lisa, for reasons known only to herself, had allowed it to go stale, crumble into dust?

He knew she'd gone through a rough time when she discovered she was pregnant with Benny, a baby they hadn't planned on having. They'd considered their family complete. They had a son and a daughter and counted themselves among the blessed.

Lisa's doctor had breezily stated that Lisa had gotten pregnant despite her use of birth control pills. It happened on occasion, the doc had said, and it was up to Lisa and Harrison to decide what they wanted to do.

Ending the pregnancy was not an option that Lisa would even consider, Harrison mentally rambled on. She'd have to have the baby, start all over again with diapers, bottles, teething woes and potty training. They'd given away the crib, changing table, all the equipment that was required for a baby and would have to once again set up a nursery.

As time passed and he'd watched Lisa grow big with the baby, he'd found himself filled with a sense of anticipation, an eagerness to once again hold their newborn child in his arms, inhale that marvelous baby aroma, take over the night feedings so he could have his private one-sided conversations with another little Parker. Another miracle.

Whenever he'd suggested to Lisa that they get started on preparing the nursery, she'd tell him she was too tired, or her back hurt, or her feet were swollen and ached even more if she didn't keep them propped up. He had finally taken over the project himself, and could still remember how hurt, how disappointed he'd been when Lisa had given the room a cursory glance and said it was fine.

When Benny had been born, Harrison remembered, Lisa had told him to just pick one of the names from the boy list they had made and that would be that. She had spent a great deal of time in bed when she and baby Benjamin came home, saying she didn't feel well, had no energy. He'd hired a cleaning lady and a baby nurse to help out until Lisa was back on her feet.

Benny was almost four months old before Lisa had rallied and taken charge of their home and the care of their three children. She seemed like herself again, devoted to the kids, to him. She seemed happy.

Had it all been a charade? Harrison wondered. A phony facade that Lisa had adopted because she felt she had no other choice? Did she feel trapped in that house, her sentence extended until she could have some freedom because she had to go back to the starting line with a newborn baby?

Was that when Lisa's cake began to crumble?

If that was true, then why hadn't he, her husband, the man who claimed to love her, sensed, known, that things were not as they should be? He had been completely besotted by his new little son, had taken over his care the minute he walked in the door at night, as well as seeing to David's and Chelsey's baths and story time.

Had he been so wrapped up in his role of father that he'd *failed* to realize that he had a very unhappy wife, who was just going through the motions of performing in her roles of wife and mother?

"Ah, hell," Harrison said, "I don't know. I'll never know."

Enough of this, he thought, shutting down the computer, then getting to his feet. It was almost 1:00 a.m.; he was bushed, and was going to bed. Tomorrow night he'd start tackling the first of the three files. After the kids were asleep and Maggie was curled up in the corner of the sofa with a book, he'd come up here and...

Maggie.

Harrison began to wander around the room, his hands shoved into the back pockets of his jeans.

This past week had gone so smoothly, he thought, it was as though Maggie had always lived under this roof. The pattern was the same each day. The kids had little to say to him when they arrived home from school, then ran to greet Maggie at the door when she got there after working at the library.

When Maggie stepped through the doorway, genuine smiles lit up his children's faces and they competed for her attention, each wanting to tell her about their day. She'd laugh, assure them that they'd all have a chance to share at dinner, then look across the room to meet his gaze.

And each night at that moment, his heart would thunder like a herd of buffalo and his mind would hum with the same message over and over. Maggie was home.

And each night as he tossed and turned in his big empty bed he became more acutely aware that Maggie was sleeping just down the hall. So close. So very close.

"That's all," Harrison said.

He smacked the light switch on the wall, left the office and strode down the hall toward the master bedroom, telling himself, as he did each night, to just keep moving past Maggie's closed door until he was safely behind the door of his own bedroom.

But as he approached the guest room where Maggie was sleeping, his step faltered as he saw a ribbon of light creeping into the hallway from beneath the door. He stopped and stared at the door, wondering why she was awake, wondering if she was ill, needed help. Needed *him*.

He raised one hand to knock, then hesitated, the loose curl of his fingers tightening into a fist until the knuckles turned white.

Yes? No? he thought. He didn't know what to do. But, damn, he had enough trouble sleeping when he knew that Maggie was snoozing away in this room without worrying that she might be sick or upset about something.

He had a responsibility as the man of this house to see to it that all was well at day's end, which was corny as hell and really a stretch to justify knocking on that door.

Forget it. He was going to bed in his own room. Right now.

Harrison rapped lightly on Maggie's door.

One second ticked slowly by, two, three...then the door was opened a fraction of an inch and Maggie peered out with one eye.

"Hi," Harrison said quietly so as not to wake the kids, "I saw your light and was concerned that you might not be feeling well."

"I'm fine," Maggie said, her voice muffled behind the door. "But thank you for asking."

"Oh. Well, why are you awake?"

"Because I couldn't sleep," she said.

"Oh. Why not?"

Because of you, you dolt, Maggie thought. She'd had difficulty getting to sleep every night since she'd moved under the same roof with Harrison Parker.

The moment she'd begin to drift off into blissful slumber, the remembrance, the vivid pictures of making love with Harrison in the private circle of rainbow lights beneath the Christmas tree would jolt her wide wake.

She was so furious with herself that she could scream. She'd been foolish to believe she was sophisticated enough to have a one-night stand—oh, how tacky that sounded—then go merrily about her business.

She'd made love with Harrison, hadn't just taken part in tension-releasing sex. Her emotions had become intertwined with the physical giving of herself to Harrison, the giving and receiving.

Tonight she couldn't stand it, couldn't toss and turn in the darkness for one second longer. So she'd turned on the light and attempted to put herself to sleep by reading a very dull book, which hadn't been working one iota.

"Maggie?" Harrison said, snapping her back to attention.

"What? I, um, was so engrossed in the book I was

reading downstairs earlier that I couldn't wait to read more. So, here I am, reading my little heart out. Okay? Sure. Good night."

Harrison frowned. "You're a lousy liar, Maggie Conrad."

Maggie flung the door open, planted her hands on her hips and glared at Harrison.

"That was a rude thing to say, Harrison Parker."

"I'm sorry but—" Harrison stopped speaking as his gaze flickered over Maggie.

She was wearing an enormous T-shirt that had slid to one side to reveal the soft skin of her shoulder and fell to mid-thigh. The weight of her hands was pulling the material taut over her breasts, outlining them to perfection, the nipples taut buttons pressing against the soft cloth. Faded letters printed across the shirt delivered the message that Librarians Do It In The Stacks.

"Oh, good grief," Maggie said, glancing down at herself.

She crossed her arms over her breasts and took a step backward.

"I'm fine. Really," she said, hearing the slight trembling of her voice. "It was just a night when I couldn't sleep. Happens to everyone at some time or another."

Harrison cocked his head to look at Maggie's bed.

"Where's the book you were reading?" he said, raising his eyebrows.

"Who made you a member of the FBI?" Maggie

said. "Is this any of your business? No, it is not. Therefore, go away." She executed a big yawn. "I'm sleepy now. Yes, I certainly am."

"Mmm."

Harrison propped one shoulder against the door-jamb and folded his arms loosely on his chest.

"I find this very interesting, Maggie," he said. "You see, I've had trouble sleeping lately myself. I just toss and turn, toss and turn. But I know exactly why that is and I think perhaps we should compare data, then maybe solve the problem for both of us at the same time."

"I don't think that's a good idea," Maggie said, then drew a quick breath as she realized she was having difficulty breathing.

"The cause of my insomnia," Harrison went on, as though Maggie hadn't spoken, "is very simple, yet it's also very complicated. You know what I mean?"

"I don't have a clue," Maggie said with a weary sigh.

"The reason I can't sleep, Maggie, is you. I think about you snuggled in that bed over there, just a handful of feet from me. I think about the night we made love in that circle of light, the rainbow water-fall. I think about how you tasted, how your soft, dewy skin felt. I recall your aroma of fresh air and flowers, and hear the little whimper of desire that escaped from your lips when I—"

"Harrison, don't," Maggie said, shaking her head. "Just don't."

"I'm not playing games with you, Maggie," he said, pushing himself off the doorjamb. "I'm being honest, open, communicating with you. I don't want there to be any secrets between us, because secrets can become lies, and after a while it's impossible to tell fact from fiction."

"I..."

"So, I'm telling you the truth, exactly what I'm feeling," Harrison said, looking directly into her eyes. "I want you. I want to make love with you.

"I thought I could handle our agreement about what we shared beneath the Christmas tree, but I can't. Not even close. I'm not pushing you, pressuring you, attempting to seduce you. I'm just giving you the facts as they stand.

"Maybe now that I've said it out loud I'll be able to sleep. I don't know. So, there you have it. I guess I don't have anything else to say. Good night, Maggie."

"'Good night, Maggie'?" she said, her voice rising. "You stand there and say all those things in a deep, rumbling voice that somehow feels like velvet caressing me, making me want you beyond measure, sentencing me to another sleepless night because I can't get you off my mind, either, then just casually say 'Good night, Maggie'?"

"That's the only option open to me," Harrison said. "Unless you want me to fling you over my shoulder and carry you to my bed, make love to you for hours and hours, then sleep so close together that our heads are resting on the same pillow and—''

Harrison shook his head. "I'm a masochist. I'm a full-blown, card-carrying masochist. I'm standing here dying by inches, going up in flames, wanting you more than I can even begin to express in words, knowing I have nothing to offer you. But my desire for you is real and honest, with no strings attached. So, yeah, all I can say is 'Good night, Maggie.'''

"So what you're saying," Maggie said slowly, "is that you want to change our one-night stand into a full-blown affair for the duration of the time that I'm living here in your house."

Harrison frowned. "That sounds very cold and clinical when you say it like that."

"I tell it like I see it, Mr. Parker," she said, matching his frown.

"Well, you're wrong. I care for you, Maggie, I do. I care for you, and about you, and I would never want to do anything to hurt you. I think you are a rare, unique and wonderful woman. I've never met anyone like you before.

"What I'm talking about here is not sex, it's making love, which doesn't mean we're *in* love with each other but we are far past hopping in bed with someone we just met in a bar.

"I like you as a person, respect you, feel ten-feet tall because you no longer seem uncomfortable in my presence like you did at first and I like that, I really do. No, I have nothing to offer you on a permanent basis because despite what you say I still believe that I failed as a husband and I never intend to take on that role again and make another woman miserable.''

"But—"

"I know, I know," he said, raising one hand, palm out, to silence her. "You believe that Lisa was responsible for her own inner peace and happiness, and I was frosting on her cake. That's a nice theory, but I happen to believe that I was instrumental in making her cake crumble.

"Look, I'm going to tell you something that might make this easier for you to understand. Benny was not planned. For some unknown reason Lisa's body wiped out, cancelled, however you want to describe it, the effectiveness of the birth control pills she was taking and she got pregnant. She was *not* thrilled, not even close.''

"She didn't want Benny?"

"Well, that's making it too personal, too harsh, because you're thinking about Benny as we know him now. Lisa didn't want to be pregnant again, have another baby. Understand?''

"Yes," Maggie said, nodding. "How did you feel about it?''

"That's where I blew it," he said, with a sigh. "Once I was over being stunned that Lisa was pregnant, I realized I was really stoked, so damn excited about having another child. I was counting down the days until I could hold that little bundle in my arms and…

"I didn't address Lisa's being terribly upset, figured she'd be fine once the baby was born and she actually saw him, held him, viewed him as the miracle he was. I failed her, Maggie, because I was so self-centered all I focused on was my own cloud-nine emotions.

"I believe that was the beginning of the end of my marriage. I believe Lisa felt isolated, lonely in her own home. I believe she began to hate me then, because I didn't come through for her.

"Eventually, she finally accepted that Benny was here and needed her just as David and Chelsey did. She was a wonderful mother to all three of them, but her love for me had been snuffed out because I wasn't there for her in a crunch situation. She needed me to understand how she felt and I didn't do that."

"Oh, Harrison."

"Lisa was talking to Justine, her best friend who lives next door, and said she wondered when we had stopped loving each other. Deep down I think Lisa knew exactly when she stopped loving me and I don't blame her one bit. She began to build a wall around herself and kids, leaving me on the outside looking in, and it took its toll, finally destroying my love for her. But the bottom line is, it was my fault. I failed her.

"If I did it to Lisa, I'd do it to another woman. Not on purpose, cripe no, but because I don't get it, don't understand how to love someone the way they deserve to be loved. I smashed Lisa's cake to smithereens and I'll never again allow myself to be in a position where I'd do that to anyone else."

"I see," Maggie said softly.

"Do you? Really? I don't want to discover what there might come to be between us, Maggie. No. I don't intend to go down that road again. I care for you, respect you, and heaven knows I want you, but as far as us having a future together? I won't even contemplate that.

"Like I said, I have nothing to offer you except what we could share while you're living here. I don't really expect that to be enough for you, and I am now going to say good-night and end this conversation."

Maggie's heart was beating so wildly she could hear the echo of its racing rhythm in her ears.

Harrison was being totally honest with her, actually baring his soul, rendering himself vulnerable to her possibly verbally attacking him, ripping him to shreds by throwing his confession back in his face, agreeing that he had been a lousy husband, a self-centered scum who didn't deserve Lisa's love and devotion.

Oh, what it must have cost him to tell her all that he had, but he'd done it for her, to be certain that he would never hurt her, not have her misconstrue what his desire for her meant, not daydream about being his wife, a mother to his children and a child they might create together.

Harrison was trusting her with his innermost secrets, the truth about himself as he perceived it, to protect her from him and his flaw—the belief that he didn't know how to properly love a woman.

What precious gifts these were that he was giving her, Maggie thought. Honesty. Truth. Trust. Whatever she decided now, in the next tick of time, would be with complete understanding. There was no future to be had with Harrison Parker. There was only the now, the days and nights ahead while she was living there in his home.

She had a choice. She could decide it wasn't enough, was too empty and stark, or she could accept things as they stood and cherish the memories when she returned to her little cottage...alone.

"Get some sleep," Harrison said, bringing Maggie from her tangled thoughts. "We're on duty with the terrible trio all day tomorrow and their Christmas break has officially begun so there are a lot of tomorrows to keep them from murdering each other. I'll see you in the morning."

Say it, Maggie, she ordered herself. Tell Harrison that she was going to sleep now and they'd rendezvous in the kitchen when the kids announced that the new day had begun. Close the door and go back to bed. Alone. Just as she'd be in the days, weeks, months, years that stretched before her. Say it, Maggie. Say "Good night, Harrison," and close the door.

"I want you, Harrison," Maggie heard herself say. "I understand everything you've said to me and I thank you for your honesty more than I can begin to tell you.

"We're on borrowed time, in a temporary situation, and I know that. I'm asking nothing of you but the chance to keep, to treasure, the memories of what we've shared while we *are* together. And then I'll leave, go back to where I belong, and that will be that.

"My only stipulation is that I don't want the children to know that we're… They've lost one mother and if they see, sense, that something is going on between us, they might fantasize about my stepping into that role and then I'll be gone soon, too. We mustn't do that to them."

Harrison nodded as he looked at Maggie intently.

"Are you very certain you can handle this?" he said. "We're talking about a short-term affair here, Maggie. There's no nicer way to put it because that's exactly what it will be."

"I'm a woman who has the right to make her own decisions, her own choices and I have." Maggie lifted her chin. "We will be friends and lovers while I'm living here, but not beyond that time. So be it."

Harrison stared at her for a long moment, then extended one hand toward her, a hand that was not quite steady.

"So be it," he said, his voice gritty.

As though standing outside of herself, Maggie saw

her hand float up, then over to lay in Harrison's palm. He curled his fingers, pulled her gently toward him, then dropped her hand to encircle her shoulders with his arm.

They walked down the hallway to the master bedroom together, entered, then closed the door on the world they were leaving behind.

Nine

Maggie stirred, opened her eyes, then wondered in her sleepy mind why she seemed to be pinned in place in her bed, unable to move. In the next instant she realized that she wasn't in *her* bed, she was snuggled close to Harrison in *his,* and one of his arms was laying across her, just below her naked breasts.

She lifted her head just enough to see the clock on the nightstand and the fact that it was a few minutes before 5:00 a.m. Lowering her head again, she gazed at Harrison who was sleeping soundly, now able to see him quite clearly as her eyes adjusted to the darkness.

Harrison looked so peaceful, Maggie thought, so free of worry and stress as he slept. But even in repose there was a rugged quality to him, his strength and masculinity not diminished by slumber.

They had shared a beautiful night of lovemaking, Maggie mused on. Harrison was such a giving, considerate lover, always making certain that her pleasure came before his own. He made her feel feminine, special, cherished. No woman could ask for more while engaged in a—

Maggie frowned.

She could scramble around in her mind for an hour, she thought, and not be able to find a word to replace the one that described what she was engaged in with Harrison Parker. She, Maggie Conrad, was having an affair.

It was such a shallow description, threatened to turn lovemaking into being merely sex. It shouted the status of temporary, of being a meaningless fling, of *doing it* as often as possible before time ran out.

She had never in her life been involved in something like this, something so out of character for her. Once she got over being nervous and intimidated in the presence of masculinity-personified Harrison, she'd really gone for the gusto.

But what she was doing, the decision she had reached, felt so right, so meant to be…for now. She could only hope that when it was over, when she returned to her little cottage, she would be content with only the memories of what she had shared with Harrison, and that the memories would be enough.

But what if—God forbid—she fell in love with Harrison during this interlude due to her lack of experience and sophistication in knowing how to keep her emotions under control?

Dear heaven, what a disaster that would be. Instead of sitting in her minuscule house, staring into space with a dreamy smile on her face for the endless days to come as she relived every moment with Harrison, she would be a miserable mess. She would be weeping in the darkness, missing Harrison to the point that her existence was nothing more than one crying jag after another and the bone-chilling truth of her loneliness.

Enough of the gloom and doom stuff, Maggie told herself. She refused to dwell on the dark what-ifs for one second longer. She was going to grab hold of every bit of bliss within her reach while she was living under this roof and tuck it carefully away in the treasure chest in her heart.

The future, whether it brought sunshine with the memories of Harrison, or a stormy cloud that would hover over her forever, would arrive eventually and there was nothing she could do in the present to change how it might be.

So, forget it. She was going to enjoy what she had while she had it, realizing she was living one step removed from reality, from her world as it really was. This fantasy place was glorious, filled to the brim with lovemaking that was pure ecstasy, a magnificent man whose attention was focused on her when they were alone, and the bright, smiling faces of three heart-stealing children.

Children, Maggie thought, who mustn't find her stark naked in their father's bed.

Hardly breathing, Maggie lifted Harrison's arm just enough to begin to wiggle from beneath its weight.

"And where do you think you're going?" Harrison said, in a deep, sleep-laden voice.

Maggie dropped Harrison's arm, resulting in a rather unladylike "oomph" escaping from her lips.

"I didn't mean to wake you," she said, her voice hushed. "But I must get back to my own room before one, or all, of the kids come bouncing in here asking what's for breakfast." She poked Harrison's arm with a fingertip. "Move this thing so I can leave."

"No."

"Yes."

"No." Harrison slid his hand up to cup one of her breasts, stroking the nipple gently with his thumb. "Even my nutso kids don't wake up this early, magical Maggie. Our private time in our private world isn't over yet."

"But—"

"Shh," he said, then shifted above her so he could capture her mouth in a searing kiss.

"Mmm," was the only sound that Maggie could make as the embers of desire within her were once again fanned into hot, leaping flames that consumed her.

She wrapped her arms around Harrison's neck, sinking her hands into his thick, in-need-of-a-trim hair, urging his mouth harder onto hers. She savored the sensuous sensations sweeping throughout her, gloried in them, rejoiced in her femininity and Harrison's incredible masculinity.

Harrison was right, she thought hazily, there was plenty of time left before the children were awake. It was still dark and they were sleeping in the cozy cocoons of their beds, far, far away. Mmm.

Maggie, Harrison's mind hummed. Oh, man, what a fantastic way to wake up and start the day. With Maggie. The night had been sensational, beyond description, and with the coming of morning she was still here, next to him, warm and soft, feminine and…his.

His? his mind repeated, as he deepened the kiss. Well, yes, she was…for now. He wasn't off-base to think like that because they'd mutually agreed to have an affair. He didn't like that tacky word all of a sudden. There had to be something else to call what he and Maggie were sharing. It was a…temporary relationship. Which translated into affair any way he looked at it. Damn.

Later. He'd think about semantics later. Because right now he was aroused to the point of near-pain, and Maggie was responding to him in total abandonment, and he wanted her, and she wanted him, and… Ah, Maggie, good morning.

He moved over her, then filled her, sensing, just knowing she was ready for him, and she was. She'd shifted her hands to his back, then lower, pressing against him, raising her hips to meet his.

Mmm.

The matching rhythm began, gaining force, thundering in a tempo that was like a wild storm raging, pounding, taking control. Harder. Faster. Their bodies one entity, meshed, synchronized to perfection. Higher. Hotter. Reaching.

Then...

"Harrison!"

"Maggie, my Maggie."

The climax was shattering in its intensity and they clung to each other to keep from being flung into oblivion. The rainbow waterfall they thought existed only in the world they'd created beneath the Christmas tree was there now, with them.

They stilled as the brilliant lights drifted over them in changing, shifting shades, then spread below to make a soft, welcoming place for them to settle onto as the last, rippling waves of ecstasy swept throughout them.

Harrison lifted himself from Maggie, then lay close to her, one hand splayed on her soft stomach that was warm and dewy under his palm.

Maggie sighed. It was a lovely sigh, a womanly sigh, a sated sigh of contentment and fulfillment.

"Me, too," Harrison said, then drew a deep, shuddering breath. "Whew. You are incredible, magical Maggie."

"No," she said dreamily. "We are incredible. Together."

"I'll go with that." Harrison's eyes drifted closed. "I'll also go with another hour of sleep. We over-thirty types have to replenish our strength after a younger woman has had her way with us."

"You are so full of baloney," Maggie said, laughing softly. "I'm really leaving this time to go back to my room. I'll remember last night and this morning, Harrison. It was so...so..."

"Yes, it was," he said. "I don't want you to go sneaking off like a thief in the night, but I guess you'd better." He kissed her on the forehead. "See you at breakfast."

"Okay."

Maggie slid off the bed, found her panties and T-shirt which she tugged on, then went to the door and opened it a crack to peer out.

"Coast is clear. Bye."

She left the room and closed the door behind her with a quiet click.

This was nuts, Harrison thought, frowning. He and Maggie were the adults in this house, yet their actions were being dictated by three little kids. Ridiculous.

No, it wasn't. Children had an uncomplicated way of thinking about things. A went to B, was followed by C and on and on.

It was like the time that Chelsey's friend Morgana's cat had kittens. To Chelsey it was very simple. A—Morgana had kittens at her house that needed a home. B—Chelsey wanted her very own kitten so...C—she'd pick her furry pet from the litter at Morgana's. Chelsey had pitched the fit of the century when he and Lisa had refused to allow Chelsey to have a kitten.

If Chelsey would have been older at the time she probably would have yelled something like "What's the matter with you people? Don't you understand the program, get the drift of how this is supposed to go?''

A went to B, then on to C.

If the Parker offspring discovered Maggie in Harrison's bed the A would be easy. A—Maggie was sleeping where Mommy used to sleep, therefore... B—Maggie was their new mommy and...C—she'd stay there with them forever and ever, unless she became an angel in heaven like Mommy had.

No, Harrison thought, he and Maggie had to be very careful about the way they conducted themselves. His kids' hearts had been torn to shreds once already by losing a mother. He couldn't, wouldn't allow them to suffer any further pain by assuming that Maggie was mother number two, only to lose her too, when she left.

When she left, Harrison mused, as sleep drifted over him. God, that was a depressing thought. So, he wouldn't think about it.

Harrison rolled onto his stomach and went back to sleep.

''Why aren't you guys smiling?'' Maggie said, as she delivered plates of scrambled eggs, bacon and toast to David, Chelsey and Benny where they were sitting at the kitchen table. ''Look out the door, the windows. There is a gazillion inches of gorgeous snow on the ground just waiting for snowmen and snow angels to be made. Why the long faces? Why aren't you excited about the first big snowfall of the year, my sweetie pies?''

"It just means we're stuck in the crummy house all day," David said, folding his arms over his chest and glaring at his plate.

"Why?" Maggie said, sliding onto a chair next to Benny.

"I told you when we were getting the Christmas tree, Maggie," David said. "Our mom doesn't— didn't want us to get cold and wet in the snow."

"I know you said that when the snow was falling," Maggie said, "but I thought perhaps your mother might have been concerned that you'd be caught in unexpected snow and you might not be dressed warmly enough." She paused. "She didn't allow you to go out and play in the snow once it was here, on the ground?"

"Nope," David said. "Never."

"I do believe," Maggie said, getting to her feet, "that I need to discuss this with your father."

"Father is here and accounted for," Harrison said, coming into the kitchen. "Hungry, too."

"I'll make you a plate of breakfast, Harrison," Maggie said, going back to the stove. "How much of the conversation did you hear about the kids not going out to play in the snow?"

"All of it, I think," he said, sitting in the chair Maggie had vacated and ruffling Benny's hair. "Hi, buddy." He looked over at Maggie. "I stopped to tie my shoe right outside the door."

"And?" Maggie said, walking toward him with a plate in one hand and a mug of coffee in the other.

"Thank you," Harrison said, accepting the offering. "Looks and smells great. Eat up, short people."

Maggie joined them at the table with a plate holding a piece of toast, several slices of bacon, and accompanied by a mug of coffee.

"And?" Maggie prompted, leaning slightly toward Harrison. "You went along all those years with the philosophy that the kids would get sick if they got wet and cold by playing in the snow?"

Harrison took a big bite of eggs, chewed and swallowed.

"Maggie, look," he said, "you have to understand something. I know zip about the care and feeding of children, even though I was a kid once myself. I figured Lisa knew what she was doing so I backed up whatever she said."

"You let them stay out in falling snow when we were selecting the Christmas tree," Maggie said.

"It wasn't coming down that hard and we weren't going to be out in it very long so..." Harrison shrugged.

"Harrison," Maggie said, "didn't you play in the snow when you were a child? Build snowmen? Go sledding? Have snowball fights, the whole nine yards?"

"Oh, yeah, I sure did," he said, chuckling. "I'd show up at the back door of my house like a bundled-up Popsicle. Frozen solid. My mittens would be covered with those icy little balls, and my fingers were so cold they wouldn't bend anymore." He paused. "I really had fun, though. My mom would just unpeel me, layer by layer and send me off to take a hot bath."

"Did you get sick from being wet and cold?" Maggie said.

"I don't remember. Maybe. I don't know."

"Well, *I* remember that I didn't get sick from playing in the snow," Maggie said. "I mean, sure, I probably had a winter cold here and there but…Harrison, maybe we should discuss this privately."

"No, go ahead with what you're saying," he said, meeting her gaze.

"You told the kids that you're in charge now," Maggie said. "So, it's up to *you* whether or not they get to go out in that beautiful, beckoning snow."

Harrison looked at each of the children in turn, seeing the expressions of hope, of anticipation on their faces.

"I think," he said, a grin breaking across his face, "it's time there was a snowman in the front yard of the Parker house. A snowman built by the Parker kids."

"Yes," David said, punching one fist in the air.

"I gotta find my boots," Chelsey said, starting to slide off her chair.

"Hold it, miss," Maggie said. "We'll all finish our breakfasts, *then* we'll find the proper gear and bundle you up. Eat."

"Are you going to play in the snow with us, Maggie?" Benny said.

"I wouldn't miss it for the world, Benny bug," she said, smiling.

Harrison waited, hardly breathing, willing one of his children to ask him if he was going to join them in the fun. The only sound in the room was the clink of forks against plates as breakfasts were consumed. A chill swept through him that was so all-consuming it was as though he had already been out in the freezing weather for hours.

"I guess you'll be glad we're outside, huh, Dad?" David said finally, not looking at his father. "You can get a lot of work done in your office because it will be quiet in here."

"Yeah," Harrison said, then took a swallow of coffee.

"How come you like work more than you like us, Daddy?" Chelsey said.

"I don't," he said, the color draining from his face. "Oh, Chelsey, believe me, I don't like work more than you three. I love you guys. I—"

"Mommy said you liked computers better 'cause they didn't talk back," Benny said. "She said you liked computers better than anything."

"Benny, that's not true. Your mother—" Lied. Damn it, she lied over and over again to their children. She made him out to be a self-centered, unloving man who didn't give a rip about anyone or anything beyond his almighty career. "Your mother was mistaken.

"I'd like to play in the snow with you three and Maggie very, very much, but I guess I'm not certain that you want me to. Nobody feels comfortable being where they're not welcome. It's up to you three as to whether or not I stay in my office and work, or join you outside."

Chelsey and Benny looked at David, who appeared totally confused, then all three of the children shifted their gaze to Maggie.

"No, I can't answer this for you," she said, shaking her head. "This is your decision to make."

Please, little Parkers, Maggie silently begged, ask your father to play in the snow with you. Her heart was aching for Harrison. It was as though she could feel his emotional pain as he once again paid the very high price for what Lisa had done. Harrison didn't deserve this. He was a devoted father who loved his children so very much.

He was convinced that he'd failed as a husband and father, but she didn't believe that for a second. He had loved Lisa until he had no more to give because she wasn't giving anything in return. He'd continued to love his children, not knowing that Lisa was stabbing him in the back whenever the opportunity presented itself.

Oh, David, Chelsey, Benny…please.

"You *really* want to play in the snow with us,

Dad?'' David said, narrowing his eyes. "Cross your heart and hope to die?''

"Stick a needle in my eye,'' Harrison said, raising his right hand as though taking a pledge.

David nodded slowly. "Cool.''

"Cool,'' Benny echoed, at three times David's volume.

"Oh, this is great, great, great,'' Chelsey said, clapping her hands. "Can we build a snowman? With a carrot for a nose and put a hat on him and all that stuff?''

"Sure,'' Harrison said, his voice gritty with emotion. "You bet, Chelsey.'' He looked at Maggie who smiled at him warmly. "Cool.''

"Way cool,'' she said, blinking back sudden tears. "Absolutely perfect.''

The snowman was a masterpiece that stood in the center of the front yard. It had three big balls for a body, tummy and head, radishes for eyes, a carrot for a nose, and a row of raisins to create its smile. The hat was a multicolored stocking cap with a matching scarf, and garden gloves hung on the ends of twigs that were arms.

"Oh, he is so beautiful,'' Chelsey said, clasping her hands beneath her chin. "This is my very first snowman in my whole long life that I ever helped build and I want to keep him forever and ever.''

"Enjoy him while he's here, Chelsey,'' Harrison

said, "because he's going to start melting when the temperature creeps up."

"I don't want him to die," Benny said, his voice quivering. "Just be gone, not here anymore, be dead 'cause he died."

"It's okay, Benny bug," Maggie said gently. "He'll be an angel in snowman heaven after he melts."

"Oh," Benny said, nodding. "That's not so bad, then, I guess."

"It's lame," David said. "When you melt, you melt."

"David," Maggie said, a warning tone to her voice.

"And go to snowman heaven and get to be an angel," David said quickly. "Got it. No problem."

"Thank you." Maggie paused. "Well, I'm frozen. Who's ready for hot chocolate? Raise your hand."

Four gloved hands shot up, the biggest one belonging to Harrison.

"Okay," Maggie said. "Let's all go in the back door so we can take off our outer clothes and boots in the laundry room, then I'll fix—"

"Hello, hello," a woman called.

"Hey, Justine," Harrison hollered. "Come see our prize-winning snowman."

Justine ran to where the group was standing, shivering as she pulled a sweater more closely around her.

"I'm not dressed right to be out here," she said,

"but I couldn't resist seeing this fine fellow you all made. Isn't he gorgeous? This is the first time there's been a snowman in this yard as far as I can remember."

"That's 'cause our mommy didn't let us play in the snow 'cause she thought we'd get sick from being wet and cold," Chelsey said, "but our daddy said we could play outside, and Maggie said we could play outside, so we did, and we made a snowman. When it melts it will go to snowman heaven."

"I see," Justine said, smiling. "Well, I'm going to enjoy him while he's here."

"Me, too," Benny said.

David frowned. "We'd better not get sick from being wet and cold."

"David, honey," Justine said, "even mothers make mistakes sometimes. Your mom was wrong about not letting you play in the snow. I even told her that more than once but..." She looked directly at Harrison. "I think maybe your mother was mistaken about a great many things. That doesn't mean I'm saying she was a bad person, she was just...just confused. Understand?"

"No," David said.

"Yes," Harrison said. "Thank you, Justine. Hearing you say that means a lot to me, considering you were Lisa's best friend."

"A best friend who has been doing a lot of thinking lately about...things, Harrison," Justine said, then smiled at the kids. "I'd say you'll do just fine if you listen to your daddy, wee ones." She shifted her attention to Maggie. "I don't believe we've met. I'm Justine Smith. I live next door."

"Maggie Conrad," she said. "I work at the library, but I'm also the...the nanny for these three for a little while."

"Maggie is a Parker right now," Chelsey said, "'cause this is a Parker snowman. Maggie has been a Parker a whole bunch of times when we've done stuff. Right, Maggie?"

A flash of the sensuous lovemaking shared with Harrison consumed Maggie's mind for a moment, and she felt a rush of heat on her cold, rosy cheeks.

"Maggie Parker," Justine said. "Well, it has a nice ring to it, I must say. Oh, I'm frozen solid. Goodbye, goodbye. I'll enjoy Mr. Snowman Parker by looking out my window from now until he melts and goes to snowman heaven. I'm gone. Cold, cold, cold."

"All right, Parkers," Harrison said, "we're headed for the back door. Let's march. All five of us."

"You got it exactly right, Daddy," Chelsey said, "'cause Maggie is a Parker again."

"Yep, she is," Harrison said. "Go."

Maggie Parker, he thought, as the group trudged through the snow toward the rear of the house. It *did* have a nice ring to it. Maggie Conrad Parker.

Harrison stopped and looked back in the direction that Justine had gone.

She'd been delivering some very heavy duty messages during her short visit, he thought. Even though she had been Lisa's best friend, she'd been letting him know that Lisa had been wrong, made mistakes. Justine had told the kids they'd do fine if they listened to their daddy.

Was it possible that Justine was realizing that Lisa had undermined his role of father? Was it possible that Justine also realized that Lisa's unhappiness had been hers to own, but that she'd built a wall around herself, making it impossible for Harrison to communicate with her, help Lisa smile again?

He knew, damn it, he knew, as each day went by that he was a good father, a devoted father who loved his children beyond measure.

Was it possible that he might very well have been, before Lisa shut him out, a good and loving husband, too? Or was he giving himself credit that he didn't deserve because Lisa wasn't there to dispute where he was coming from?

Hell, he didn't know. Decent dad? Yes, he was.

Capable of loving a woman the way she deserved to be loved? He was still very shaky about that one.

The problem was, he thought, starting toward the back of the house again, he'd better figure it out pretty damn fast. Yeah. Because he was slowly but surely falling in love with magical Maggie.

Maggie Conrad…Parker.

Ten

The following day Maggie took the kids shopping for Christmas presents for their teachers and father, Harrison slipping her some money before they left the house.

They stood in the middle of the crowded mall, Maggie watching as frowns settled onto all three of the children's faces.

"What's wrong?" she said.

"We never did this before," David said. "Our mom used to buy stuff for Dad and the teachers, then we wrapped it. We didn't go with our mom to pick out the presents or anything."

"Old news," Maggie said, flapping one hand in the air. She was finished defending Lisa Parker, of explaining gently that things were different now, or that even mothers made mistakes and blah, blah, blah. Enough was definitely enough. "You'd better put on your thinking caps."

"We get to pick whatever we want to give our teachers and our daddy?" Chelsey said, her eyes widening.

Maggie laughed. "Within reason, sweetie pie. We should have gotten the presents for your teachers before school let out for the holidays, but you can take them the gifts the first day back after the break. Let's start by window-shopping.''

"I don't want to buy a window," Benny said.

"Oh, man," David said, rolling his eyes heavenward. "You don't buy the window, Benny, you look through it to see the junk."

"Oh." Benny nodded. "'kay."

Chelsey selected a bright red scarf for her father and a paperweight for her teacher that had a snowman inside. When it was tipped over, snow fell from an invisible sky.

Benny wanted the same paperweight for *his* teacher, then insisted that his daddy needed a pen that had three colors of ink, each available by pushing the proper button.

David chose a box of pretty stationery for his teacher, but rejected everything he saw that might be a gift for his father.

"I'm tired of doing this," Chelsey said finally, then stuck her thumb in her mouth.

Maggie pulled the thumb back out, then looked at David.

"Haven't you seen anything you like, David?" she said. "We're putting a lot of miles on our piggy toes."

"Yeah, well, I liked that coffee mug but maybe it's lame." He shoved his hands into his jacket pockets and stared at the floor.

"The mug you were holding in that store back

there?'' Maggie said. ''The one with the printing on it that said 'World's Best Dad'?''

''Yeah,'' David said, his head still bent.

Oh, good grief, Maggie thought, she was going to cry. David was telling his father so much by wanting to give him that mug. What a wonderful, beautiful gift. What wonderful, beautiful children. Oh, how she loved them, all three of them, and she loved their father, and she—

''What?'' she said aloud. ''What?''

''Forget it,'' David said. ''It was a dumb idea.''

''Oh, no, no, David,'' Maggie said quickly. ''It's not dumb, it's super. Come on. We're going right back there and get that mug. It's perfect, more than perfect. It's a great mug, a fantastic gift and—''

''How come you're talking so fast, Maggie?'' Chelsey said. ''You're going to run out of air or something.''

Maggie pointed to the store where the treasured mug was waiting and the trio headed in that direction, a jangled Maggie following behind.

She was not in love with Harrison Parker, Maggie told herself frantically. She'd just been caught up in the sentimental and momentous event of David wishing to let his daddy know that all was forgiven, that Harrison was a good father, a special father, the best father in the world.

It had been a heart-tugging moment and made her realize how much she had come to love these children, then because she was on temporary emotional-overload caused by a coffee mug, she'd lost control and zoomed right on to blithering in her mind that she loved their father as well.

Which wasn't true.

No, of course it wasn't.

She cared for Harrison...a lot. Respected him. Ached for him for the injustices done to him by his deceased wife, who had chosen a dark path and taken their children with her.

But she wasn't in love with Harrison, for mercy's sake.

Maggie sighed in defeat and registered the sudden urge to go running through the crowds and out the main entrance of the mall, never to be seen again. But there was nowhere to run from the truth, nowhere to hide.

She was in love with Harrison Parker. Deeply, irrevocably, forever and ever, in love with Harrison. She'd lost her heart to a man who didn't want it, which was a guarantee that said heart would be smashed to smithereens and there would be no one to blame but herself.

"This one," David said, picking up the mug.

"Huh?" Maggie said, pulling herself from her tormented thoughts. "Reach to the back of the display there, David, and get one of the boxes. We'll pay for the mug and head for home."

"But, Maggie," Chelsey said, "we can't go home yet. You didn't buy Daddy a present."

I gave him my body and he went on to steal my

heart, Chelsey, Maggie thought, with an edge of hysteria. Isn't that enough?

"You're right," she said. "Any suggestions?"

The trio just stared at her.

"Thanks a lot," she said. "Come on, David, let's go pay for the mug."

Back in the center of the mall, Maggie told the children that since everyone was tired, she'd shop for her gift for their father on another day.

"We're not *that* tired," David said. "What are you going to buy him?"

"I don't have a clue," Maggie said, grabbing Benny's hand and starting off.

They went into and out of four stores, with Maggie just shaking her head.

And then she saw it, and her heart skipped a beat as her breath caught.

It was a five-by-seven-inch print matted with a smoky shade of blue. It was a picture of a waterfall cascading into a pool below that was edged by trees with the sun peeking through the branches. Where the sun's rays shone, the waterfall was transformed into a glorious, multicolored rainbow.

With hands not quite steady, Maggie picked up the print, her mind overflowing with exquisite and treasured memories of making love with Harrison in the rainbow lights beneath the Christmas tree, in that wondrous, mystical circle that had belonged only to the two of them.

What would Harrison think she was attempting to

tell him by giving him this gift? What *was* she trying to say? Maggie wondered. She didn't know, she didn't care, she just knew she was meant to give him this print. She had to. Why? She didn't know that, either, but since she was losing her mind, what was one more unanswered question thrown on the muddled mess that used to be her brain?

"What's he going to do with a picture of water?" David said, frowning.

Benny stared at the print. "I have to go potty."

"He'll remember to take a shower," Chelsey said, appearing very pleased with herself that she'd figured it out.

A strange-sounding little bubble of laughter escaped from Maggie's lips, which, she immediately decided, was better than bursting into tears and scaring the poor kids to death.

"No more comments, please," she said, poking her nose in the air. "I'm buying this for your father. The subject is closed. Follow me to the cash register, then we're going home. After dinner tonight we'll all meet in my room and wrap these presents. Any questions? No? Good."

The trio eyed Maggie warily, then followed her to the counter in single file like little ducklings.

That night after the children were in bed, Maggie retrieved the library book she was reading from her bedroom and started back down the hall. She hesitated outside the half-closed door of Harrison's office, the house so quiet she could hear the clicking of the computer keys as he typed.

She'd been edgy and nervous ever since she'd returned from the shopping trip, ever since she'd discovered during that outing that she was in love with Harrison Parker. She could only hope that he hadn't noticed her strange behavior.

Maggie rapped lightly on the door.

"Come in," Harrison said.

Maggie entered the room, returned the door to its halfway point, but didn't move closer to where Harrison was sitting in the chair in front of the computer.

She didn't remember this room being this small, Maggie thought. She didn't remember that the masculine essence of Harrison seemed to fill it to overflowing, weaving around her, stroking her, making her heart thunder and prompting desire to thrum deep within her.

"Maggie?" Harrison said.

"Oh. Sorry. I was off somewhere. I apologize for disturbing you, Harrison, but I have a quick question."

"And I have a question for you," he said. "But ladies first."

"I just wondered what you'd bought, or were planning to buy, for the kids for Christmas so I wouldn't duplicate anything you might already have gotten them."

"Oh," he said, then told her what gifts he had already purchased.

"Okay. Thanks. I'll let you get back to work,"
Maggie said, looking at a spot in space a few inches
above his head.

"Wait a minute," Harrison said, getting to his feet.
"I said I had a question for you, remember?"

"Oh, yes, you did say that, didn't you? Well, fine.
You just go right ahead and ask me whatever it is
that's on your mind."

Harrison closed the distance between them and
frowned as he met Maggie's gaze.

"What happened?" he said. "I feel like the clock
got turned backward. You're as jumpy around me as
you were when we first met. Ever since you came
back from the mall you've been acting weird. Is it
me? Did I blow it somehow? Do something to make
you uncomfortable again?"

"Oh, no, no," Maggie said. She watched in horror
as her right hand floated upward on its way to Harrison's rugged cheek. She snatched it back and folded
both hands around her elbows. "You haven't done
anything wrong, Harrison. I was tired from the shopping spree, that's all. Out of steam. I've gotten a second wind now, though, and I'm fine, good as new."

"Why am I having a hard time believing that?"

"I have no idea," she said, lifting one shoulder in
a shrug. "Nope. Not a clue. Perhaps your imagina-
tion is working overtime."

Maybe he *was* just imagining that Maggie was acting strangely, Harrison thought, because *he* was different. He was a man in love, who wasn't certain he

had the right to be in love, didn't know if he was capable of loving a special woman like Maggie the way she deserved to be loved.

"Mmm," he said, nodding slowly.

"So, how is the project going?" Maggie said.

"Very slowly," he said, dragging one hand through his hair. "I narrowed it down to three files I found that I was unable to get into. I broke the code on one and it wasn't what I was looking for. The second had a firewall protecting it and so far I can't break through it."

"Is there any way I could help you?" Maggie said. "I know a little about computers because I keep an inventory of the children's books at the library on the computer. I'm certainly not even close to having your expertise but I'd be willing to help if there was something I could do."

"Really?" Harrison said. The little bit she saw wouldn't reveal what the project was about and, besides, he trusted her. "No, that's not fair to you, Maggie. This quiet time when you read belongs to you. You've been with the kids all day while I've been in here working. You should relax, put your feet up, read your book."

"I really wouldn't mind, Harrison."

Why was she doing this? Maggie asked herself. Did she have hidden masochistic tendencies she hadn't known about? Why wasn't she hightailing it downstairs to the safely of her little corner of the sofa, putting distance between herself and Harrison?

Why? Because she loved him, wanted to be with him, close to him, assisting him with his project if she could, for as long as possible before she returned to her cottage and faced the bleak reality of the lonely future stretching before her.

"Well, if you're positive," Harrison said. "I could sure use an extra pair of eyes. I'm trying to compare the printout of the program to this file with what is presented on the computer screen. Layered codes often show up in a hard copy."

Maggie nodded. "That sounds like something I can handle."

But could *he* handle being with Maggie in this minuscule room, Harrison thought, wondering how she might feel about him, torturing himself with the question of whether he had any right to hope that her feelings for him might be growing, matching his for her.

Maggie gave of herself so completely when they made love. But what about her heart? Did she still have a solid firewall around her heart?

"Okay," he said, forcing a lightness to his voice that he definitely wasn't feeling. "Let's do it, partner."

Partner, his mind echoed. Soul mate. Wife.

Partner? Maggie thought. Like a wife? The other half? A soul mate?

At midnight, Maggie yawned.

"Harrison," she said, "these strange little squiggles are all starting to run together in a blur. I'm afraid I just can't do any more of this tonight.''

"Oh, hey, I'm sorry," he said, turning in his chair to look at her where she was curled up in an old easy chair. "Time just got away from me. That happens when I'm doing computer work. I don't think about anything but what I need, what I— God, I'm a jerk. Go to bed. Get some sleep. I really apologize for wearing you out like this and—"

"Halt," she said, holding one hand palm out like a traffic cop. She handed the printed sheets to Harrison, then folded her hands in her lap. "You've got to quit being so hard on yourself, Harrison."

"What do you mean?" he said, swiveling the chair around so he could look directly at her.

"You were convinced that you were a crummy father," Maggie said quietly, "and it's been proven to you time and again that it just isn't true.

"Yes, okay, maybe you weren't connected with your children for the months immediately following Lisa's death, but in the big picture you're a wonderful father and the important thing is, your kids are coming to realize that. They love you, are rebuilding a foundation of trust in you.

"The majority of their negative attitudes were instilled in them by Lisa. I'm sorry if you don't like to hear me speak poorly of her, but facts are facts. She did you a terrible injustice and it's being set to rights, a step at a time. David, Chelsey and Benny *do* love you very much."

"Thank you," he said. "It means more than I can express to you to have you say that."

"It's the truth," Maggie said. "But…"

"But?"

"You also came to believe that you weren't an adequate husband, that you didn't know how to love Lisa enough to make her happy, and because of that flaw you think you have your marriage was destroyed."

"I…"

"Harrison," Maggie went on, "I'm not saying that what happened to you and Lisa, the fact that there just wasn't anything left between you to build on, nurture, is entirely her fault. But by the same token it's not entirely your fault, either. But your misplaced guilt is causing you to doubt yourself to the point that you overreact to things."

"What do you mean?" he said, frowning.

"Like right now," Maggie said. "I said I was tired. Goodness, that's a reasonable thing for me to say after a long day. But you immediately started beating yourself up about my fatigue.

"I'm exhausted because I chose to keep working when I should have stopped. It was my decision, not yours. When something isn't exactly as it should be, you jump to the conclusion that it's your fault. I own my mistakes, Harrison. They don't belong to you."

Harrison nodded slowly.

"If you don't move past this business of taking the blame for everything, a special woman you might meet is going to be uncomfortable, won't be able to relax when she's with you because she'll be afraid that she'd make some remark that will cause you to fall all over yourself apologizing to her when she never intended for you to feel guilty."

Maggie got to her feet.

"Well, now that I've totally minded your business, which was very rude of me, and went on and on like a person with years of relationship experience, which I'm not, I'm going to bed before I fall asleep in the middle of one of my ridiculous sentences. Good night, Harrison."

Harrison sank back in his chair. "Good night, Maggie. Thank you for your help with the project and...well, for caring enough for saying what you did. Sleep well."

Maggie nodded and left the room.

Harrison stared into space, replaying in his mind every word that Maggie had said. He sat there for a full hour, deep in thought, until he finally realized what time it was. He shut down the computer, turned off the light in the office and went to bed, falling immediately into a deep, thoroughly exhausted, dreamless sleep.

The next day they all went to the mall, with Harrison taking the children shopping for gifts for Maggie, while she headed in the opposite direction in search of presents for the kids.

She got David a book about dinosaurs. Chelsey's

gift was a tea set fit for the princess she would become when she wore the outfit from her father. And
precious Benny bug's present was a cowboy outfit
and a pair of pajamas that would fit the stuffed Velveteen Rabbit that he was getting from his daddy.

Maggie glanced at her watch when she returned to
the agreed upon meeting place and saw that she was
early. She sank onto a wooden bench and hugged the
bags containing the treasures.

What she had done, she thought, frowning, was to
purchase gifts for the kids that complemented,
matched up with, the presents Harrison had selected
for them, which was overstepping her place in the
Parker family beyond measure. It was pushy and borderline rude. But for this Christmas, just this one, she
was a Parker. So be it.

She wiggled into a more comfortable position on
the hard bench and waited for her temporary family
to arrive.

On the other end of the mall, three short Parkers
were staring up at one tall Parker.

"Well, Dad," David said, "it's your turn to buy
a present for Maggie. I got her a pair of mittens.
Chelsey picked that smelly soap. Benny decided
Maggie needed that little tiny china Velveteen Rabbit. So…"

"So, we're almost out of time," Harrison said,
looking at his watch. "We have to meet Maggie

pretty soon and we don't want to keep her waiting. I'll shop for my present another day."

"No," the trio said in unison.

"Oh," Harrison said.

"Jeez," David said. "We just went through this with Maggie wanting to put off getting *your* gift. I hope you pick something better for her than she got for you."

"I like what Maggie got Daddy," Chelsey said.

"It makes me have to go potty when I look at it," Benny said.

"It what?" Harrison said, staring at his younger son.

"Forget that," David said. "Come on, Dad. Maggie will understand if we're a little late meeting her."

"You guys are ganging up on me," Harrison said. "Okay, okay, let's hit the stores again."

They marched in then out of four shops, then Harrison looked in the window of the fifth and nodded.

"That's it," he said. "It's perfect."

"What? What?" Chelsey said.

"It will be lame, believe me," David whispered to his sister. "Maggie's gift to Dad sure is."

"It makes me have to go—"

"We know, Benny," David said. "Hurry up. Dad is way ahead of us and it's crowded in there."

The children found Harrison in front of a display of shawls that were so soft that Chelsey said she bet that was what clouds in the sky felt like.

"The pink one," Chelsey said. "I like pink."

"Oh, no, not pink, Chelsey," Harrison said, carefully lifting a shawl from the table. "Blue. This is the same shade of Maggie's eyes. It really is. She can wrap it around her when she's reading a book and she'll look so beautiful in a shawl that matches her eyes to perfection. She has the prettiest eyes I've ever seen and this shawl will make them even more—"

Harrison stopped speaking and cleared his throat as he felt a warm flush creep up his neck. He looked down at his children who were all staring at him as though they'd never seen him before in their life.

"Yeah, well, whatever," he said, shrugging. "It's a nice gift, which means I'm finished shopping, which is not my favorite thing to do in the first place so... Do you guys have a problem?"

"Your voice was all gooey when you were talking about Maggie's eyes," David said, "and how beautiful she'll look in that shawl and— Wow."

"My voice was not gooey, David," Harrison said, then glanced around quickly as he realized he'd been speaking much too loudly.

"Yes," Chelsey said, nodding slowly, "it was. Gooey. Like in *Sleepless in Seattle* when they meet on the top of that big building after a zillion years and say hi, and tell their names and stuff, and look at each other and kind of smile but not exactly. Their voices are gooey. That's 'cause they know they love each other. And Jonah, too. They love that little boy, Jonah."

"Do you have anything you'd like to contribute to

this conversation, Benjamin?'' Harrison said, ignoring the heat on his neck that was definitely still there.

''I have to go potty,'' Benny said.

''Why?'' David said. ''Because the blue shawl reminds you of water so you think you have to go potty?''

''Guess so,'' Benny said, shrugging.

''We'll find a bathroom in a minute, Benny,'' Harrison said. ''Let me ask you something, children of mine who are aging me before my time. Suppose, just suppose, that my voice *was* gooey when I was talking about Maggie's eyes and blah, blah, blah. How would you feel about that?''

''Gooey voices are good, very good, Daddy,'' Chelsey said. ''It would mean that you love Maggie, and that would mean you could marry her, and that would mean we would have a mommy again, and that would mean—''

''Cut,'' Harrison said. ''Thank you for your input. David?''

''Well, see,'' David said, ''the first time we watched *Sleepless in Seattle* Mom was there in the living room with us and we had popcorn and stuff, and I thought it was a dumb movie.

''But then we watched it again after…you know, after Mom was an angel in heaven, and it made my throat hurt like something was stuck in there because Jonah was going to have a new mom because his mom was an angel in heaven, too. I didn't think it was a dumb movie anymore. I wished, just for a minute, that I was Jonah. Maggie sure would be a way cool mom, Dad.''

''Way cool mom,'' Benny echoed.

''We need to listen real careful,'' Chelsey said, her voice hushed as she looked at David, then Benny, ''to see if Maggie ever talks in a gooey voice about Daddy.''

''Right,'' David said, narrowing his eyes. ''Got it.''

''What I've got is a headache,'' Harrison said. ''This topic is closed. Stick close to me so you don't get lost while I pay for this shawl.''

''I need to go potty,'' Benny yelled. ''Right now!''

''Oh, for crying out loud,'' Harrison said, striding toward the front of the store.

Eleven

To Maggie, the following busy days, and the exquisitely beautiful lovemaking nights with Harrison, seemed to fly by. She had a mental image of the scene often used in old movies where a calendar is shown with the pages being ripped away by an invisible hand and flung into oblivion.

While David, Chelsey and Benny were moaning that Christmas was *never* going to get here and why couldn't time go faster, Maggie was silently wishing that time would simply stop so she wouldn't have to face the dwindling number of hours left until her stay at the Parker home was over.

More snow fell, creating a sparkling fairyland. Maggie and Harrison taught the kids how to make snow angels, prompting Justine to join them, saying she was watching from her window and just had to be part of the fun.

One afternoon was spent with Maggie and the children making Christmas cookies. Before going upstairs to his office to work, Harrison had magnanimously offered to clean the kitchen after the baking spree since he fully intended to eat his share of the goodies.

The Parker offspring were enthusiastic bakers, and Harrison groaned aloud when he saw the condition of the kitchen when he reappeared. To the laughing delight of Maggie and the kids, Harrison stuffed a cookie in his mouth, rolled up his sleeves and scrubbed and rubbed the kitchen until it shone.

A shopping trip to the grocery store was made after a family meeting to determine the menu for Christmas dinner. A turkey with all the trimmings were purchased, with Harrison overloading the cart with snacks, which were needed, he said, to properly watch the multitude of football games scheduled over the holidays.

Days ticked steadily away, one after another.

On the night before Christmas Eve, Maggie lay snuggled close to Harrison in his bed, both of them sated and contented after sharing beautiful lovemaking. Harrison sifted his fingers through Maggie's curls, relishing the feel of the silky texture.

"Oh, I forgot to tell you," Harrison said, breaking the peaceful and comfortable silence.

"Hmm?" Maggie said.

"When I went to the post office today, I stopped at the store and got stuff to give the kids from Santa Claus. You know, for their stockings. Candy, boxes of crayons, little stuff, so the Santa thing is covered."

"Does David still believe in Santa Claus?" Maggie said.

"No, but he goes along with it for Benny and Chelsey. Actually, I think Chelsey figured out that

Santa isn't real but she's pretending for another year. It's a difficult fantasy to let go of. I figure whatever works for her is fine with me.''

"You're a super daddy, Harrison,'' Maggie said, fiddling with the damp swirls of hair on his broad, hard chest.

"Thank you, ma'am. I'm giving it my best shot.''

"Well, you're doing a wonderful job,'' Maggie said.

Yeah, Harrison thought, he felt good about his role of father to his children. He sure wasn't perfect, but he was seeing more smiles than frowns from David, Chelsey had stopped sucking her thumb, and Benny chattered like a magpie.

Sure, part of their change of attitude was due to Maggie being there, but he wanted, needed, to believe that he was adding to the vastly improved atmosphere within the walls of their home.

If only he felt such confidence in the role of husband. He loved Maggie so much, just so damn much. He wanted to marry her, hold her in his arms as he was doing now every night, wake up next to her in the morning. He wanted to create a baby with Maggie, watch her grow big with his child.

But, oh, God, what if, despite his love for her, he just didn't come through for Maggie? What if he couldn't love her the way she deserved to be loved? What if he hurt her, made her cry and—

"Harrison, what is it?'' Maggie said. "I can feel how tense you've gotten all of a sudden.''

"Nothing, nothing," he said. "My mind drifted to my work, shame on me, and it's so frustrating that I haven't found what I need in those coded files that—Forget it. I'm not dwelling on that while I have you in my arms and—"

A sudden piercing scream cut through the air and both Harrison and Maggie jerked in surprise, then sat bolt upright in the bed.

"Benny," Maggie said, scrambling off the bed and reaching for her robe. "He's having a nightmare. Oh, poor Benny bug. I thought he was over those."

Maggie ran from the room as Harrison tugged on his robe, then followed close behind her.

In Benny's room, Maggie snapped on the lamp on the nightstand.

"Maggie, Maggie, Maggie," Benny screamed, tossing his head on the pillow, his eyes closed. His hair was damp with sweat and he was clutching the blankets in tight little fists. "Where…you…go, Maggie?"

"Benny," Maggie said, gripping his shoulders and nudging him gently. "Benny bug, wake up. It's Maggie. I'm right here, sweetheart. Open your eyes and you'll see me."

Benny's eyes shot open and in the next instant he launched himself into Maggie's arms, nearly toppling the two of them off of the bed. He flung his arms around her neck and held on for dear life.

"I couldn't find you, Maggie," Benny said, sobbing. "I looked and looked, and you were gone and—"

"Shh," she said, rubbing his back. "I'm here. I'm here."

Harrison stared at the pair, his heart racing.

Benny had a nightmare centered on not being able to find *Maggie?* Not Lisa, but Maggie? he thought. Had Benny moved past the loss of his mother, gotten closure somehow about Lisa, and was now focused on the new mother-figure in his life? Yes, that was apparently what had happened.

Was this good? Harrison wondered, dragging a restless hand through his hair. Well, yes, time had healed the wounded heart of his youngest son. Of course, that was good, it was great.

Hell, he could understand why Benny loved Maggie because he, himself, loved her beyond measure, and he had a sense, a feeling, that David and Chelsey felt the same. They'd sure gotten all excited when he'd talked about Maggie in a *gooey* voice, for Pete's sake.

But, oh, man, what if his now blissful children were let down again by their father? A father who was not convinced he knew how to love Maggie in the proper manner. What if Maggie walked out of their lives because Harrison Parker had nothing of substance to offer her?

"There you go," Maggie said gently, easing Benny back down to his pillow. She brushed his hair from his forehead. "You're fine now, Benny. It was just a dream. It wasn't real. I'm not lost where you can't find me, I'm sitting right here on your bed.''

"Stay with me," Benny said, grabbing her hand.

"For a little bit," she said. "Just until you're asleep again, then I'm going back to—" Maggie cleared her throat. "My own bed.''

"'kay," Benny said.

"'kay," Harrison echoed, then smiled warmly at Maggie when she turned to look at him. "Thank you for…well, a long list of things. Good night, Maggie." He reached down and wiggled Benny's toes. "Good night, sport. I love you, Benny."

"I love you, too, Daddy," Benny said, his lashes beginning to flutter as sleep crept over him. "I love you too, Maggie."

"And I love you, Benny bug," she whispered, feeling the ache of threatening tears in her throat.

Harrison turned and walked slowly from the room, taking the lovely image of Maggie and Benny with him.

On Christmas Eve, Maggie and Harrison waited until they were certain that all three of the kids were finally sound asleep, then gathered the wrapped gifts from closet shelves and placed them beneath the tree next to the presents the children had put there earlier in the evening.

"We're ready," Maggie said, nodding. "The stockings are filled, the treasures are waiting to be opened, the turkey is ready to go in the oven tomorrow, and the kids and I prepared as much of the other food that could be done ahead of time. I tell you, Harrison, this is a well-run ship.''

Harrison slipped one arm across Maggie's shoulders and nestled her close to his side as they continued to gaze at the rainbow lights on the sparkling tree.

''You,'' he said, dropping a quick kiss on the top of her head, ''are a marvel. Magical Maggie. I don't know what I—what any of us—would have done without you over the past days. You've staked a claim on a lot of hearts in this home.''

Including yours? Maggie yearned to ask, but lacked the courage.

You've captured my heart, too, Maggie Conrad, Harrison thought, but I'm too shaky, too unsure of myself to tell you that.

''You're not going to work tonight, are you, Harrison?'' she said, looking up at him. ''On Christmas Eve?''

Harrison sighed. ''Yeah, I'd better. Matt desperately needs the information I'm trying to find. I will, however, not enter my office at all tomorrow, day or night. Christmas is a family day and I'll be front row center.'' He paused. ''Oh, man, I hope the kids like what I bought them. I am admittedly nervous about that. If they hate the gifts the day is blown.''

''Tsk, tsk,'' Maggie said. ''There's that lack of confidence in yourself again. They will love the presents you selected for them, you'll see. They love you, too, Harrison. I hope you no longer have doubts about that.''

"No, I think it's there, their love for me. The trust in me had to be reestablished first, that's for sure, but I believe it's pretty solid again. With the foundation of trust back in place, their love has somewhere solid and steady to grow. We're doing okay.''

"Now you're talking," Maggie said, smiling.

"Maggie," Harrison said, "do you realize the significance of the nightmare Benny had? We didn't talk about it later, but the fact that he was calling for you, was terrified because he couldn't find you—not Lisa, you—says a helluva lot.''

"Yes, it means that Benny has made great strides in putting the grief over the loss of his mother to rest,'' she said, nodding. "That's good. I think the other two are doing the same. I can't remember the last time they even mentioned Lisa's name. It's been many, many months since they lost their mother and time has worked its wonders.''

"Let's sit down," Harrison said.

They settled on the sofa, Maggie curled up next to Harrison, her legs tucked next to her and her head on his shoulder.

"There's more happening than the kids moving past their grief for Lisa," Harrison said. "Benny's dream, things the other two have said all indicate that they love you, see you as the mother-figure in their lives.''

Maggie raised her head and shifted slightly away

from Harrison, staring at her hands, now clutched in her lap.

"Oh, I'm not convinced that's true, Harrison," she said softly. "They know, understand, that I'm only here temporarily. As soon as the holiday break from school is over, I'll be returning to my job at the library. You'll find a nanny, or housekeeper, or whatever you want to call her and…that will be that."

"It won't be the same without you here, not for any of us," Harrison said, covering her hands with one of his. "You've become a…well, a Parker, like Chelsey said way back when. You're part of this family, Maggie."

"Temporarily," Maggie said, a sharp edge to her voice as she got to her feet, then turned to look at Harrison. "In another week or so, I'll be gone.

"I won't be a Parker anymore. I'll be Maggie Conrad, children's librarian, living in my little cottage and— I really don't see any point to this conversation, Harrison. Facts are facts, and if you're concerned about the kids' feelings for me I think you're underestimating them. They know I'll be leaving soon."

Harrison narrowed his eyes as he studied Maggie.

"You sound angry all of a sudden," he said.

"No, no, I'm not angry," she said, wrapping her arms around her elbows. "I'm having to face the same facts that the kids are and it's difficult. My time here with them and what I've shared with you have been wonderful, so very special. But, damn it, Harrison, it's temporary. I know that, you know that, your children know that. There's no point in discussing it.''

Please, Maggie thought frantically. She couldn't talk about this. She couldn't chat about when she'd be gone, when this fantasy world she'd been living in would be pushed aside by the stark loneliness of her reality. She couldn't stand there and look at the man she loved with her whole heart, the very essence of who she was, and verbally count down the days, hours, minutes that were left to be with him. No.

''I...I think I'll go to bed now, Harrison,'' she said. ''Tomorrow is going to be a big day and I have a feeling it's going to start quite early in the morning. It would be best if I just went to my own room now, because we don't know when the kids might wake up and announce that Christmas has officially begun.''

''I've upset you somehow, haven't I?'' Harrison said, getting to his feet.

''Don't do that,'' Maggie said. ''Don't take the blame for *my* emotions that are out of control at the moment. You didn't do one thing wrong. Believe in yourself, Harrison. You're not just a great father, you're a fine and honorable man and I— Good night. I'll see you in the morning.''

Maggie turned and hurried from the room.

''Good night, Maggie,'' Harrison said quietly when she was upstairs. ''I'm working on believing in myself. I really am. Ah, God, Maggie Conrad, I love you so much.''

Harrison stood in front of the Christmas tree for several long, memory-filled moments, then turned out the lights and trudged slowly up the stairs to go to his office and attempt once again to crack the code on the files and find the information Matt needed about Gideon.

"Oomph," Harrison said, his eyes flying open as a wiggling weight settled on his chest.

"Wake up, Daddy," Benny said. "It's Christmas, and Santa came and put stuff in my stocking, and we gotta open presents. I didn't touch anything. I just peeked in the living room and I saw. Come on, Daddy, you gotta get up now."

Harrison turned his head enough to look at the clock on the nightstand.

"Benny, it's five-thirty in the morning," he said, with a groan.

"That means you better hurry 'cause it's getting later and later," Benny said, tugging on Harrison's T-shirt. "Chelsey is waking Maggie up, too, and David said he'd go turn on the lights on the Christmas tree and—"

"Okay, okay," Harrison said, laughing. "Could you get off my chest, so I have a fighting chance of getting out of this bed without broken ribs?"

"'kay," Benny said, scrambling off the bed and

running across the room to drag Harrison's robe from a chair and bring it to him. "I'm helping."

"That you are," Harrison said, swinging his feet to the floor but staying seated on the edge of the bed. "Merry Christmas, Benny. I love you whole bunches."

"I love you, too, but come on," Benny said, tugging on his father's arm.

Harrison emerged from his bedroom in his robe to find Maggie tying the sash on hers in the hall with Chelsey urging her to hurry, hurry, hurry. Maggie turned to smile at Harrison and their gazes met for a warm, special moment.

"Merry Christmas," Harrison mouthed.

"You, too," Maggie mouthed in response, then looked at Chelsey. "I'm coming as fast as I can, sweetheart."

"I know that old people can't move as fast as kids," Chelsey said, "but really try hard this time. Okay?"

"Oh, good grief," Maggie said with a burst of laughter. "Old people? Harrison, you need to have a talk with your daughter. She'll be packing us off to a nursing home at the rate she's going."

Whatever works as long as we're together, magical Maggie, Harrison thought, then shook his head in the next instant. Brother, he was really a goner when it came to this enchanting woman.

They came down the stairs to find the Christmas tree glowing and David standing next to it, the brightest smile Maggie had ever seen on his face welcoming them to the living room.

"Merry Christmas, David," Maggie and Harrison said in unison, then laughed in surprise at their perfectly coordinated greeting.

But the tone was set. It was laughter and smiles, squeals of delight as the festive paper on carefully wrapped presents was torn away to discover the hidden treasures beneath.

Harrison realized that he was hardly breathing as his children opened the very first Christmas presents he had ever bought them, then felt tears prickle his eyes as they gave rave reviews to what they had received.

"I'm a princess, I'm a princess, I'm a princess," Chelsey said, twirling round with the wand in her hand. "I'm the most beautiful princess in the whole wide world."

"Cool. Oh, man, way cool," David said, when he saw his huge 3-D dinosaur puzzle. "Thanks, Dad. This is totally awesome."

"You're—" Harrison said, then cleared his throat, "You're very welcome, son."

Benny buried his face in the soft Velveteen Rabbit, hugging it so tightly that Harrison feared the stuffing might pop through the seams.

The trio opened the gifts from Maggie next, and the presents were received with the same enthusiasm. Harrison looked at Maggie when he realized that she'd coordinated her gifts to match his, his heart nearly bursting with love for Maggie Conrad.

Maggie and Harrison were presented with their gifts from the children, and Harrison got to his feet when he saw the mug from David, unable to keep his raging emotions under control for another second.

"I'll be right back," he said, his voice husky. "I've got to go start a pot of coffee since I have such a spectacular mug to drink out of."

Maggie opened her presents from the kids and hugged each of them in turn, telling them she had never received such wonderful gifts.

When Harrison returned to sit on the sofa by Maggie, David placed the gift from Harrison to Maggie in her lap, then did the same with the present from Maggie to Harrison. The three little Parkers sat cross-legged in front of Maggie and Harrison, their expressions intense, their eyes riveted on the adults.

"Well, my goodness," Maggie said, "what can this be?"

"Open yours first, Maggie," Chelsey said.

Maggie nodded, then slid one finger beneath the tape on the pretty paper and brushed it back to reveal the exquisite blue shawl. Her breath caught as she ran her fingertips over the soft material.

"It matches your eyes," Chelsey said, leaning slightly forward. "Dad said it did. That's why he bought it. He said you'd look beautiful when you wore that shawl to read a book, and that you had the prettiest blue eyes he'd ever seen in his whole long life.''

"How very, very special," Maggie said, hardly above a whisper as she met Harrison's gaze. "I'll *feel* beautiful whenever I wear this because you picked it out for me. Thank you so much, so very much, Harrison."

"She did it," Chelsey yelled, then flopped backward onto the carpet. "Maggie's voice was gooey when she talked to Daddy just now about the shawl. It was, it was, it was. Gooey, gooey, gooey."

"What?" Maggie said, tearing her gaze from Harrison's and staring at Chelsey, obviously confused. "Gooey? Did you say gooey?"

"Don't go there, Maggie," Harrison said, rolling his eyes heavenward.

Chelsey popped back up. "Yeah, gooey. See, Daddy's voice was all gooey when he was talking about the shawl and your eyes and stuff, and that means—"

"Chelsey," Harrison interrupted. "Put a cork in it. I'm going to open my present from Maggie now."

Harrison tore off the paper, dropped it to the floor, then held the print of the waterfall with the gorgeous rainbow in both hands, which were trembling slightly. He shifted his gaze to the place beneath the tree where he'd first made love with Maggie in the private circle of colored lights, then looked at Maggie, who was staring at him, her lips pressed tightly together as she waited for his reaction.

"I will treasure this," he said, emotion ringing in his voice, "for the remainder of my days. Thank you, Maggie, more than I can even begin to tell you."

"You're welcome," she whispered, managing to produce a rather quivering smile. "I'm so glad you like it, Harrison."

"They're both doing gooey now," David said, close to Chelsey's ear. "Cool."

"Why aren't they saying the I-love-you stuff," Chelsey whispered to her brother, "instead of the thank-you stuff?"

David shrugged. "Big people do a lot of things that are sort of dumb and don't make sense. Maybe they don't say the I-love-you stuff until there aren't any kids around to hear them."

"Oh," Chelsey said. "Well, they let us hear the gooey junk."

David shrugged again.

Benny crawled forward and looked at the picture his father still held in both hands.

"Don't let him look at it, Dad," David said, "or he'll be yelling his head off about needing to go potty. That really makes me nuts."

"Gotta go." Benny jumped to his feet and ran from the room.

"And I gotta go put that turkey in the oven so it will be ready for when we have scheduled our scrumptious Christmas meal," Maggie said, getting to her feet.

She placed the shawl on the sofa, ran her hand over it, then turned and hurried to the kitchen.

"David," Harrison said, "get a trash bag, sport, and we'll clean up the paper. This room looks like a tornado came through here."

"Then can I dress up in my princess clothes," Chelsey said, "and have a tea party, and be beautiful and—"

"Yes," Harrison interrupted with a laugh. "All of the above. As soon as we set this room to rights, I'm going to have some coffee in my new mug."

"You really like it, Dad?" David said, no hint of a smile on his face.

"Oh, yeah, David. I really, *really* like that mug."

David nodded as he smiled, then he got to his feet and went to get a trash bag.

It was a day made up of memories to keep, of smiles and laughter, delicious food, tummies being patted with the declaration that far too much was eaten but finding room for pumpkin pie in the next moment.

It was a day of a giant 3-D dinosaur growing bigger piece by piece on the living floor, a soft rabbit being toted everywhere and a beautiful princess pouring tea.

It was a day of warm gazes being exchanged between a man and a woman who were filled with the joy of the season and the fact that they were there, together, watching happy children play with their new treasures.

It was Christmas. It was glorious. And through it all, Maggie was once again a Parker, part of the family that had created a day so special they would all tuck the precious memories safely away to remember in the days ahead.

The hours ticked by so fast, so fast, and Christmas was almost over.

But it would not be forgotten. Ever.

Twelve

While Maggie had read enough articles on the subject to know that many people suffer from emotional letdowns after the holiday season, she herself had never experienced the post-Christmas blues.

Until now.

From the moment she opened her eyes the morning following the festive day, she felt as though a gloomy, dark cloud was hovering above her. There was no escaping from the fact that there were only a handful of days remaining of her stay at the Parker home.

It was strange, Maggie thought, as she entered the kitchen to make breakfast, how a person could be fully aware of how things stood and knew from the start of whatever it was, and still be thrown off-kilter by the harsh reality of it.

Princess Chelsey ran into the kitchen wearing her frilly outfit.

"Hi, Maggie," she said. "Am I still beautiful?"

"You are the most gorgeous princess I have ever seen," Maggie said, smiling at her. "Are you sure you want to eat breakfast in your finery? It would be awful if you spilled something on your gorgeous gown.''

''I'll be very, very careful,'' Chelsey said, sliding onto a chair and smoothing her skirt. ''Princesses don't spill stuff.''

''Oh.'' Maggie laughed. ''Okay.''

Harrison, David and Benny arrived with Benny toting his rabbit, and the group was soon consuming eggs, bacon and toast. It was decided that all three could invite friends over to play with the understanding that they would have to stay inside. There was a misty rain falling, the sky was rapidly filling with more ominous-looking clouds and it was bitter cold.

''Whoa,'' Harrison said. ''I have to work, Maggie. You're letting yourself in for a mob. You'll have six kids to keep tabs on in here.''

''No problem,'' Maggie said, smiling. ''Kids are on the list of my favorite things.''

''You have a favorite things list?'' Chelsey said. ''What's on it besides kids?''

Maggie propped her elbows on the table and cradled her coffee mug in both hands.

Your father is at the very top of that list, sweet Chelsey, she thought. In fact, Harrison Parker deserved a list all of his own as being the man she would love with her whole heart for the remainder of her days.

''Maggie?'' Chelsey said.

''Oh, well, let's see,'' Maggie said. ''My list of favorite things. Books to read, flowers to smell, babies and puppies to cuddle, bigger kids like you three, chocolate candy with cherries in the middle...and on and on.''

And a beautiful blue shawl, she mused.

''Cool,'' David said. ''We should get a puppy.''

''No,'' Harrison said, then took a bite of bacon.

''Well, if we can't get a puppy,'' Chelsey said, ''we should have a baby. I really like babies. I'm going to make a list of my favorite stuff and put babies on there just like Maggie did on her list. Can we get a baby, Daddy?''

''You can't buy a baby at a store,'' David said. ''Jeez. Little kids make me crazy sometimes. We'll go to the mall and buy a baby. Right. Get a brain, Chelsey.''

''I have a brain,'' she said, sticking her nose in the air. ''A princess brain.''

''Where do you get babies?'' Benny said. ''I really want a puppy, but a baby would be okay, I guess.''

''You have to have a mom and a dad,'' David said. ''They hug and kiss a lot and stuff, and then the mom gets really fat and after a long time, there's a baby.''

''Really?'' Benny said, frowning.

''Trust me,'' David said. ''I'm a lot older than you are, Benny, and I know all about these things.''

''Eat your breakfast,'' Harrison said.

''Good idea,'' Maggie said.

''Well, Daddy could be the dad person,'' Chelsey said, ''and Maggie could be the mom person, then they could kiss and—''

"Who wants more juice?" Maggie said, jumping to her feet.

"I have to get to work," Harrison said, rising.

Maggie headed for the refrigerator and Harrison strode out of the room.

She opened the refrigerator and stared unseeing at the contents.

A baby, she thought. A baby created with Harrison. What a wonderful image that was in her mind's eye. She'd be the mom person and Harrison would be the dad person and— Oh, Maggie, stop it. She was torturing herself, wasn't being her own best friend.

She closed the refrigerator, rolled her eyes heavenward and opened it again to retrieve the juice.

Harrison took the stairs two at time, went into his office and turned on the computer. He sank onto his chair and sighed.

A baby, he thought. A miracle. Another little Parker he and Maggie would create in the darkness of night in their private world. God, what a fantastic picture that painted in his mind. The mom person standing close by the dad person. Maggie Parker. Maggie Conrad Parker. Mrs. Harrison Parker. And their children, David, Chelsey, Benny and their newborn baby. So right. So perfect.

What had Maggie been thinking when the kids had gotten on their baby kick a few minutes ago? Did she care enough for him, maybe even love him, to the point that she'd imagined that baby as being one they'd made together?

He knew Maggie had deep feelings for him because she wouldn't make love with a man unless she did. He was certain of that. But was she in love with him as he was with her?

Hell, he didn't know and he couldn't exactly come right out and ask her. Do you love me, Maggie? You do? Hey, cool. Of course, it doesn't mean squat because I'm such lousy husband material I can't offer you more than the affair we're engaged in right now. But, hey, it's nice to know you love me and—

"Ah, Parker, shut up," he said, then shifted his attention to the computer.

The day was a huge success and a good time was had by all the children who filled the Parker home to overflowing with laughter. When the mothers came to collect their offspring, they each in turn extended invitations to repeat the event at their houses the next day. The Parker kids were delighted and Maggie promised to deliver the guests in the morning.

That night Maggie once again helped Harrison with the assignment from Matt Tynan after the kids were asleep. During the first half an hour that they worked, Maggie became aware that Harrison's mind was not totally focused on what they were doing.

He's here, but he's not here, Maggie thought, after repeating an answer she had already given Harrison. He was definitely preoccupied about something of extreme importance, enough to pull his mind from the project at hand.

"We just did that line," Maggie said. "The data on the screen matches what I have here in the print-out." She paused. "Harrison, you're obviously having difficulty concentrating on this tonight."

Harrison sighed and sank back in his chair, a deep frown on his face.

"You're right," he said, swiveling the chair around so he could see Maggie. "Look, you go on to bed. You had an army of kids here today and you must be bushed. I'll tackle this on my own this time."

"But—"

"It's really terrific of you to be willing to help me with this frustrating thing. I'm not going to keep you up late after the tough day you've had when I'm not even doing my part."

Harrison got to his feet, took the printout from Maggie's hand and dropped it onto the chair he'd vacated. He drew her up into his arms and kissed her deeply.

"Go," he said, his voice gritty when he finally released her. "I'll plug away at this for a couple more hours."

"Well, okay, but...Harrison, would you like to talk about whatever is on your mind? I'd listen, you know."

"No, no," he said quickly. "But thanks for the offer. I'll see you in the morning."

Maggie nodded, then crossed the room, stopping at the door to look back at Harrison for a moment with an expression of concern on her face. She left the office, leaving the door open a few inches as usual so Harrison could listen for the kids.

Harrison sank onto his chair, swore under his breath as he realized he'd just crushed the printout, then rose to pace around the small area.

Maggie had read him like an open book, he thought, picking up almost immediately on the fact that he was definitely having trouble concentrating on the project. That was putting it mildly. He was on mental overload and had nothing left for Matt's project…not tonight.

Harrison tossed the wrinkled printout onto his desk and once again settled in the leather chair. He dragged both hands down his face, then stared into space.

He was coming unglued, he thought. All he could think about was Maggie, how much he loved her, how he wanted to marry her and spend the remainder of his days with her, have a baby with her.

In a few days, just a handful of hours, Maggie's stay there at the house would be over and he did *not* want her to leave. He was rapidly running out of time to gather enough courage to declare his love and ask her to marry him. He wanted, needed, to do that while she was living under this roof, was a Parker, per se.

If Maggie didn't love him with the same intensity

that he loved her, that was okay. It was. If she loved him even a little, then that love could be nurtured, would grow, would soon match how he felt about her. She cared for him, he knew that, had no doubt in his mind that it was true. And she loved his kids, interacted with them day in, day out, as though she was their devoted, loving mother.

Everything was in place for him to reveal his feelings for Maggie and ask her to be his wife.

Everything except his courage to open his mouth and express all that he had bottled up inside of him. He couldn't seem to get through, over or go around the solid, taunting wall that screamed the fact that he had been a lousy husband when he was married to Lisa.

When things had gotten rough between him and Lisa, he'd quit, just came and went as though he rented a room there instead of being the husband of the woman who had worn a wedding band that matched the one on his finger.

What if he did that again? Did that to Maggie? What if at the first sign of trouble, the first glitch, he shut down and backed away, instead of talking things through, finding a solution to whatever had caused a bump in their road?

Maggie continually told him to have confidence in himself as a father, as a husband. The father thing was doing fine. The role of husband terrified him because he was scared to death that he would fall short, hurt Maggie, cause her to cry in the darkness of night.

But if he wanted to have Maggie in his life for all time he was going to have to reach deep within himself, believe in himself somehow and lay all his cards on the table.

Yes, he knew that the destruction of his marriage to Lisa was her fault as well as his. But that didn't erase the fact that his half of that failure belonged to him. He had to own that, take responsibility for it, bear the crushing weight of the guilt it created within him, the fear that he'd repeat his mistakes because he just didn't know how to get it right.

Harrison got to his feet again and wandered around the room.

I love you, Maggie, he mentally practiced saying. I love you and I want to marry you. No, that was no good. Okay. I love you, Maggie, and I'm asking you to marry me, be my wife, the mother of my three kids and create another little Parker with me. I have a crummy track record as a husband, but I think I'm getting a handle on it. I'm not sure and I'm scared spitless that I'll blow it, but would you take a chance on a loser and—

"Ah, hell," he said. "As David would say, that was really lame."

Harrison glanced at the computer where the screen saver of swimming fish now shone in brilliant underwater colors.

He couldn't work on the project for Matt tonight, Harrison thought, he just couldn't. He was going to go to bed, and when he woke up in the morning he'd have a special delivery message from his subconscious telling him exactly what to say to Maggie, how to put it, how to express, like a pro, how he felt.

Tomorrow was the day. It was custom-made for this life-changing discussion with Maggie, because the kids would be gone for hours and he wouldn't be broaching such an important topic late at night when both he and Maggie were tired.

Tomorrow.

How did that saying go? Harrison thought as he went through the process of shutting down the computer. Tomorrow is the first day of the rest of your life. No joke. A life that would be rich, full and wonderful, because he'd spend it with Maggie. Or a life that would be fulfilling as a father, but bleak and empty and lonely as a man.

Tomorrow.

At just after ten-thirty the next morning, Harrison brushed back the curtain on the window in his office and watched Maggie turn into the driveway after delivering his brood to their play dates. His heart thundered in his chest and a trickle of sweat ran down his chest.

His subconscious was a dud, he thought, dropping the curtain back into place. Of course, with the few snatches of sleep he'd been able to get as he tossed and turned, it hadn't exactly had the opportunity to compose his smooth, confident speech to Maggie. He was on his own, accompanied by the tight fist of fear in his gut.

Heaven help him, because tomorrow was here.

Harrison drew a deep breath, let it out slowly, squared his shoulders and strode from the room.

Downstairs he found Maggie on her knees with a pitcher, pouring water into the container on the stand holding the Christmas tree. Holiday carols played softly on the stereo.

"Maggie?" he said.

"Oh, Lord," she said, nearly dropping the pitcher. "You scared me to death, Harrison." She backed out from beneath the tree and got to her feet. "I didn't hear you come into the room. Is the stereo too loud? Disturbing you while you work?"

"No, not at all. I couldn't even hear it upstairs. I…Maggie, I'd like to talk to you and this is…this is the time to do it because the kids aren't here."

"Oh. Well, sure. Go ahead."

"Could we sit down?"

Maggie placed the pitcher on the bright red tree skirt, then crossed the room to sit down on the sofa, looking up at Harrison questioningly after she was settled. He sat on an easy chair across the room from her.

"You have the floor," she said, smiling. "Actually, you have the floor, the ceiling and the walls because this is your house." Maggie frowned as Harrison's super-serious expression didn't change. "Little attempt at humor there, which obviously didn't make the grade. I have a feeling that this is going to be a tad more serious than your saying you can't tolerate one more meal made from turkey leftovers.''

''Yeah.'' Harrison propped one ankle on his opposite knee, dropped his foot back to the floor in the next instant, then jerked his foot up to resume the original position. ''I want to discuss— No, I want to tell you that I— What I mean is— Ah, hell.'' He stared up at the ceiling, muttered a very earthy expletive, then looked at Maggie again.

''Harrison, what is it?'' Maggie said, sitting up straighter on the sofa.

''Okay, here I go, because today is tomorrow.''

''What?'' Maggie said, obviously confused.

Harrison dragged both hands down his face, then patted the air with his palms, attempting to calm down, gain control of himself.

''Maggie,'' he said finally, ''I believe you'd agreed with me that we get along great together. Right? Right. I know you care for me because you're not the type of woman who would— What I mean is you wouldn't— That is—''

''I wouldn't make love with you unless I cared for you very much,'' Maggie said. ''Yes. That's true. I won't pretend that it isn't.''

''Good, that's good, and I—I care for you very much, too,'' he said.

I love you, Maggie, so damn much, he thought frantically. I'm going to tell you that right now. I am. Maggie Conrad, I love you beyond measure, and

want to marry you, and spend the rest of my life—
God, he couldn't do this. If he declared his love for
her it was as though he was making her a promise to
be the kind of husband she deserved to have and he
just didn't know if he knew how to do that.

"I..." Harrison said, then cleared his throat.
"Look, what we have going here is great. You and
I...care for each other, the kids are crazy about you,
we interact like a family and...stuff. So why end it
when your vacation is over? You and I... Well, you
and I could get married and things could continue on
as they are. It would be a perfect solution for everyone, don't you see? I... Well what do you think?"

I think my heart just shattered into a million pieces,
Maggie thought, struggling against threatening tears.
Harrison wanted them to get married? Because they
cared for each other? Because things were running
so smoothly with her there? He was presenting a
grand gesture of making an honest woman of the
nanny-housekeeper person because it suited his pur-
poses to have her there?

Dear heaven, didn't he realize how cold and clinical he sounded? Where were the words from his
heart? The declaration of his love? All she was getting was a message from his organized brain that saw
the situation as it now stood as convenient, working
well.

They'd just keep on keeping on, with a piece of
paper showing them to be man and wife thrown in

for good measure so the gossipmongers wouldn't have a field day when she stayed on there.

Oh, God, she couldn't bear this. She'd never find all the pieces of her broken heart, never put them back together as they had been. Harrison didn't love her. He cared for her—big macho deal—and liked the way she ran his house and interacted with his kids.

That wasn't enough to base a lifetime on. It wasn't. She wanted, *needed,* the man she was in love with to love her in kind…and he didn't.

"So, um, Maggie?" Harrison said, wiping a line of sweat from his forehead with one thumb. "Will you? Marry me?"

"No," she said, hardly above a whisper. "No, I won't marry you, Harrison."

"Why not?" he said, leaning forward. "Everything is in place, isn't it? We care for each other, respect each other, you and the kids are great together and—"

"No," Maggie said, nearly yelling. She got to her feet. "If you have to ask why not, then you just don't understand what really must be in place for two people to marry. No, I won't marry you and I won't—can't—stay here another minute because you—"

Tears filled Maggie's eyes.

"You…just don't…understand. Tell…tell the kids I caught the flu and thought it best to go home a few days early so they wouldn't get it. The moms will be bringing them back about four o'clock and...I'm leaving, Harrison. I have to go. Now."

Harrison got to his feet. "No, wait. Don't go. Maggie, please don't go. We'll talk this through. Okay? Please? Maggie, I—"

"There's nothing more to say," she interrupted, a sob catching in her throat. "Don't come near me, Harrison. Don't touch me. I'm leaving. I can't bear to—"

Maggie ran from the room, then up the stairs.

Harrison curled his hands into tight fists and closed his eyes as he dropped his chin to his chest.

Dear God, he thought, he'd blown it. His fears had overpowered him, controlled what he'd said, what he *didn't* say. He'd lost his courage. He'd lost the woman he loved with every breath in his body. He had no one to blame for this but his cowardly self. Ah, Maggie, Maggie.

Unable to move, hardly able to breathe, Harrison stood where he was, his heart aching, a cold emptiness consuming him. A few minutes later he heard Maggie run down the stairs, the front door open, then close behind her.

Maggie was gone.

Harrison stumbled across the room and sank to his knees by the Christmas tree in the magical circle where he'd made love to Maggie for the first time. Unshed tears caused a painful ache in his throat and he threw back his head and called to the woman he loved who could no longer hear him.

''Maggie.''

His anguished-filled voice seemed to echo through the house, then pound against him, beating against his body, his heart, his very soul.

Maggie was gone...forever.

She would never know how much he loved her because he didn't have the courage to tell her. He was a failure, a loser, an empty shell of a man. She deserved far better than what and who he was. She knew that. And so, she was gone. Forever.

Harrison staggered to his feet, then made his way slowly across the room and up the stairs.

He would get to work now, he thought foggily. He was good at that, the work he did. Then later the kids would come home and he'd be a daddy. He was good at that now, too, being a father.

But as a man? He was nothing, and because of that he would have nothing as a man for the remainder of his days.

Because Maggie was gone.

Thirteen

The play date moms had spoken on the telephone and agreed that one of them would pick up and deliver all three Parker children home. Just after four they came bursting through the front door. Finding the living room empty, they ran into the kitchen to discover Harrison setting the table for dinner.

"Hi, Dad," David said. "Man, you should have seen the cool video games I got to play today. Awesome."

"I had fun, too, Daddy," Chelsey said. "We played dress up, and made a castle with blankets over a card table and stuff, and I had red Jell-O with whipped cream on top and everything."

"I played with a train, Daddy," Benny said. "It fell off the tracks a bunch of times, but that was okay really, 'cause I know how to put trains on tracks and it made a toot noise when it went by the station thing."

"I'm glad you all had a fun day," Harrison said quietly, setting the last spoon in place.

"Where's Maggie?" David said. "I want to tell her about the video games I played. Do we have to eat turkey again? Isn't it all gone yet?" He paused and frowned. "Dad, you didn't set enough places at the table. You only did four and it's supposed to be five. Whoa. You had a senior moment, Dad."

"Let's go into the living room," Harrison said. "I need to talk to you guys."

"Okay, but where's Maggie?" David said.

"Living room, David," Harrison said.

They went into the other room, and Harrison inwardly cringed as David stopped to plug in the tree lights.

"Sit down," Harrison said, gesturing toward the sofa.

The trio plunked onto the sofa and Harrison sat on the chair across from them, the same chair that he'd used when he'd had the devastating discussion with Maggie hours before.

"Okay," Harrison said, then drew a deep breath and let it out slowly. "Here it is. Maggie…Maggie wasn't feeling well and thought it best that she go on home so she wouldn't give you the flu or whatever it is that she was coming down with. She said to tell you that she enjoyed being here very much and she'd see you soon at the story hour at the library."

David jumped to his feet. "What? Maggie just packed up and left? Didn't wait to say goodbye to us?"

"Like I said, David," Harrison said, "she wasn't feeling well and—"

"That's bogus," David yelled. "If Maggie thought she was sick she'd stay in her bed in her room here so we wouldn't get her germs. Then she'd feel better and come back out and— She wouldn't just leave without— What did you do to make her leave, Dad? What did you say to her that made her go?''

"Daddy made Maggie leave us, David?" Chelsey said, her bottom lip trembling. "Why did you do that, Daddy? We love Maggie and we wanted her to stay here and be our mommy. Why did you send her away? I want Maggie to be with us forever and ever and ever." She burst into tears.

"I want Maggie ever and ever," Benny said, then stuck his thumb in his mouth.

"I…" Harrison said.

"Did you make her cry, Dad?" David hollered. "Did you make Maggie cry just the way Mom cried a bunch of times? Did you? I know you did. I hate you. Everything was great, and you wrecked it. I hate you more than anything."

David ran from the room and thundered up the stairs, the sound of his bedroom door being slammed reverberating through the air.

Harrison got to his feet. "David! Come back down here so we can talk about this calmly and— Ah, hell." He shoved one hand roughly through his hair.

"Maggie doesn't like to hear bad words in this house," Chelsey said, then sniffled.

"I know. I'm sorry I said that," Harrison said, slouching back onto the chair. "Benny, please take your thumb out of your mouth. That's Chelsey's number."

Benny shook his head, the thumb firmly in place.

"Look, I know you're upset that Maggie left," Harrison said. So was he. If he thought it would make him feel any better he'd stick his thumb in his mouth and cry, too. David hated him again. Well, that wasn't far off the mark. He wasn't exactly thrilled out of his socks about himself, either. "But we know how to get a meal on the table now, and how to keep things picked up and the house in order. We're a good team."

"Not without Maggie, Daddy," Chelsey said, her eyes glistening with tears. "She's the mommy person and we need her here. We need a mommy, Daddy, we do. We really do. If you made Maggie sad and she cried and stuff, can't you say you're sorry so she'll come back? You always tell us we should say we're sorry when we do crummy stuff."

"Sometimes it's just not that simple, sweetheart," Harrison said, his voice gritty with emotion. "Grown-up mistakes, the crummy stuff, are bigger, much bigger, than kid crummy stuff. Saying sorry doesn't always fix things."

"Can't you try?" Chelsey said. "Say sorry a hundred zillion times to Maggie for what you did to make her cry?"

"Chelsey, I told you that Maggie didn't feel well and—"

"I think she didn't feel well 'cause she was sad," Chelsey said, folding her little arms over her chest. "I don't want to talk to you anymore."

"Dandy. Just great," Harrison said, getting to his feet. "I'm going to make dinner, and we're all going to sit down and eat it like the family we are."

A half an hour later, Harrison put three glasses of milk on the table, then went to round up the kids. The living room was empty. He trudged up the stairs and knocked on David's door.

"Dinner, David," he said. "Now."

"I'm not hungry."

Harrison opened the door to see David sprawled on his bed.

"Downstairs at the table in three minutes, sport," Harrison said. "It's not open for discussion. Do it. And wash your hands first."

Harrison marched a thumb-sucking Benny and a pouting Chelsey down the stairs and into the kitchen. David arrived and slid onto his chair, a stormy expression on his face.

"So, David." Harrison spooned some corn onto all of their plates. "Tell us about these video games you played today."

"No," David said.

"Okay," Harrison said, slapping a slice of turkey on all four plates. "Share your fun time with us, Chelsey, about playing dress-up."

"No," she said, pushing her plate away.

"Benny, you played with a cool train, huh?" Harrison said. "Did it have a caboose?"

Benny popped his thumb out of his mouth. "Yeah,

a caboose. It was red and had little windows and back porch and stuff. It—''

''Don't talk to him, Benny,'' David said. ''You little kids have short, dumb memories. Dad made Maggie leave us, remember?''

''Maybe she wanted to leave us,'' Benny said in a tiny, quivering voice. ''Maybe she was tired of being a mom person, just like Mom was tired of being a mom person. Mom didn't want to be a mom person anymore, so maybe Maggie didn't neither.''

Oh, God, Harrison thought, they were killing him. They were ripped up, his innocent little kids, shredded. What could he do, say, to make this better somehow? This was all his fault. His cowardly, spineless fault. He loved Maggie Conrad and he hadn't had the courage to tell her that. He was blown away, his kids were destroyed...and Maggie? Was Maggie crying?

''If you don't want dinner you may be excused,'' Harrison said quietly. ''I won't make you sit here with me and eat.''

David slid off his chair and ran from the room.

''I'll eat with you, Daddy,'' Chelsey said. ''You look sad, too. Everybody is sad.''

''Everybody sad,'' Benny said, nodding.

In a foggy haze of misery, Harrison went through the motion of the evening. He supervised Benny's and Chelsey's baths, read *The Velveteen Rabbit* to them twice, which felt like a knife piercing his heart each time he turned one of the crisp pages of the book, then tucked them in and told them he loved them.

David's door remained closed. Harrison stood in front of it for a long moment, raised his fist to rap, then shook his head and walked slowly down the hall to his office.

What would he say to David if granted entry to his room? he thought, turning on the computer.

You're right, sport, I blew it with Maggie. I said all the wrong things, upset her so much that she couldn't bear to be under the same roof with me a minute longer, and so she left. Maggie is gone, David, and it's all my fault, because I'm a prisoner of my own fears and inner doubts about myself. Your old man is a dud, David, and there isn't going to be a mom person in this house for you, Chelsey and Benny. Not ever. We'd better get a puppy because there sure as hell isn't going to be another Parker baby around here.

Because Maggie is gone.

With a weary sigh, Harrison forced himself to shift mental gears and concentrate on the maze on the computer screen.

Matt was counting on him, he thought. He was going to crack this code, by damn, because he was going to come through for someone at least.

An hour later, Harrison stiffened in the chair as he stared at the screen. He glanced quickly at the printout, nodded, then slowly, very slowly, pressed one key, then another, then hesitated and narrowed his eyes as he pressed the third. The computer hummed, the screen went blank, then in the next instant the name Proteus flashed in a steady rhythm, then faded to reveal the name Medusa, then Achilles.

"Achilles," Harrison whispered, his heart beating wildly. "That's Gideon." He punched a fist in the air. "Yes! We did it, Maggie," he said, spinning his chair around. "You and I together found—"

The empty room seemed to taunt Harrison with its silence and a shiver coursed through him. He turned back to the computer, retrieved the paper with Matt Tynan's numbers and lifted the receiver to the telephone. Matt picked up on the first ring and Harrison told him what he had discovered. During the next fifteen minutes, they concentrated on Harrison forwarding the files of data on Code Proteus, and Matt acknowledging that he had received them.

"Thank you doesn't cut it, buddy," Matt said, "but thank you. You have no idea what you've done. This is fantastic. I knew you could do it, Harrison, if anyone could."

"It's nice to know I'm good at something," Harrison said.

"Hey, you don't sound like a guy filled with Christmas cheer," Matt said. "Were the holidays rough without Lisa?"

"No, Christmas was fine, really great, in fact," Harrison said. "I'm just...tired. This was a helluva project you gave me."

"I realize that. You should treat yourself to some

time off and enjoy those kids of yours. As far as this project goes, we can now concentrate on finding Gideon because of you.

"We were fairly sure, but we're now *very* positive, that no other genetically engineered children were produced by the Coalition because Gretchen, one of the Proteans, was able to break the code on her father's scientific notes. With what you just gave me we're on the road to finding the last of the original children—Gideon.

"Thanks again, Harrison, and have a happy New Year," Matt said.

"Same to you, Matt, and I wish you every success in finding this Gideon you're looking for. Good night."

"See ya."

Happy New Year? Harrison thought, as he replaced the receiver. What a joke. The new year that was rapidly approaching was a bleak picture in his mind. So empty, so lonely, without Maggie.

Well, he'd have to gear up, put on a false front because it wasn't fair to his kids to go around acting like he felt. There would be smiles and laughter in this house in the coming year, by damn. Somehow. Enough of this. He was exhausted. The emotional rush at cracking the code on the hidden files was gone, slam-dunking him into a dark, gloomy pit. He'd check on the kids, then go to bed and hope he could sleep.

And hope he wouldn't dream about Maggie.

Harrison shut down the computer, then tucked blankets more securely around Chelsey, Benny and the rabbit. He opened David's door quietly, allowing the hall light to cast a dim glow over the bed.

The empty bed.

Harrison slammed his hand against the light switch, and stared wide-eyed at David's bed that hadn't been turned down. He strode across the room, yanked open the closet door, then hurried to every room, his heart beating so rapidly it was actually causing a physical pain in his chest. He ran down the stairs and searched everywhere for his missing son.

"Oh, God, David," Harrison said finally, standing in the living room and dragging trembling hands down his face. "When did you leave? I didn't hear you go. Where are you, David? *David.*"

Harrison sank onto a chair, his mind racing.

It was so cold outside, he thought. Raining. David was out there in the dark, alone, so upset. Where was he? Where would he go?

He sat bolt upright.

"Maggie," he said. "David knows where the love, the warmth, the sunshine is. We drove by where she lives that time and...David is braver than his father-the-coward because he went after what he wants and needs."

Harrison lunged to his feet and strode into the kitchen, yanking the receiver off the wall phone. He got information, then punched in the numbers with more force than was necessary.

* * *

Maggie had postponed going to bed, not wishing to face the long hours of the night tossing and turning. She'd wept until she had no more tears to shed, ate a bowl of cereal for dinner, then sat curled up in the corner of the sofa, flipping through the pages of an old magazine and not comprehending one thing she was seeing.

The evening dragged on with Maggie just sitting there in a haze of misery. She finally scooted lower, resting her head on the arm of the sofa as she continued to turn the pages in the magazine one after the next.

She had just dozed off when she was startled bolt upright by the ringing of the doorbell, which was followed an instant later by the shrill summons of the telephone.

She jumped to her feet, the magazine falling to the floor, her eyes darting back and forth between the front door and the telephone on the end table.

"Wait," she told the telephone, then ran to the door. "Who is it?" she yelled.

"David," came the muffled reply.

"David," she said. "David?"

Flinging open the door, her eyes widened as she saw a very wet David standing on her minuscule porch in the cold, swirling rain, his hands shoved into his jacket pockets and his shoulders hunched against the freezing temperature. Maggie grabbed the front of his soggy jacket, hauled him inside the little cottage, then slammed the door.

"Stay," she said, then rushed to answer the still ringing telephone. "Hello?"

"Maggie? It's Harrison. I'm sorry to disturb you, but please, please, tell me that David is there. He ran away, Maggie, and I'm praying he's with you, because if he isn't then... Is he there?"

"Yes," Maggie said, glancing over at a shivering David. "He just arrived two seconds ago, soaked to the skin and freezing to death. What's going on?"

"Is that my dad?" David said. "I don't want to talk to him, and if he comes over here I won't go home with him. I won't, Maggie."

"I heard that," Harrison said, sighing. "Oh, God, now what do I do?"

"Harrison," Maggie said, "I'm caught in the middle here, totally confused. Give me a chance to talk to David."

"This isn't your problem," Harrison said. "I'll see if Justine can come over and stay with Chelsey and Benny, then I'll come get David."

"No," Maggie said firmly. "If David walked all the way over here in this awful weather, it's obvious that he's upset about something. Carrying him out of here isn't going to solve anything. Let me to talk to him. Please?"

"Well...yeah, okay," he said. "I'm not surprised that he went to you because... You'll call me back?"

"Yes. Yes, I will. Bye." Maggie dropped the receiver into place and hurried over to David. "Don't say a word. I'll give you a jogging suit of mine to put on after you've had a warm shower. *Then* we'll talk.''

''Is my dad on the way over here to get me?'' David said, narrowing his eyes.

''No. He's waiting for me to call him back. Come on, David, you've got to get out of those clothes and get warm and dry before you get sick.''

''You're not sick, are you?'' David said. ''That was a bunch of bull. You left us because my dad upset you, made you cry and stuff. Right? I hate him, Maggie. He ruins everything.''

''Shh. Not now. First things first here, sweetie.''

''Okay,'' he said sullenly.

Fifteen minutes later David was sitting on Maggie's sofa sipping a mug of hot chocolate and wearing a faded sweatshirt, sweatpants and a pair of Maggie's socks.

''Better?'' Maggie said, sitting down next to him. ''I put your clothes in the dryer so they'll be toasty warm.''

''I'm not going home, Maggie,'' David said. ''Not ever. Can I live with you? Please?''

''Whoa,'' Maggie said, raising one hand. ''Let's slow down here. Start at the top and tell me what's wrong, what happened, why you ran away.''

''I know my dad did something to make you leave us, Maggie,'' David said, struggling against threatening tears. ''He made my mom cry and I know he made you cry. He wrecked stuff with you just when we were a happy family again with a mom and a dad.

"We—me, Chelsey, Benny—we miss you, Maggie. We thought you were going to stay with us and be our mom. We really did. We were going to get a baby instead of a puppy and everything, then my dad messed it all up.

"We came home from our play dates and you were gone, and he said some lame thing about you being sick and not wanting to spread germs, and that was so bogus. Well, fine. I'm not going back there. Ever. I'm just going to stay here and live with you. I mean, if you let me. I'll pick up my underwear and junk and be really quiet and—"

"David," Maggie interrupted, "listen to me. I'm at fault here, too. I told your father to tell you three that I had the flu. *I* did that, and it was wrong. I should have stayed and said a proper goodbye to you, instead of just disappearing like I did. I'm sorry I did that. I'm so very sorry."

"Oh." David frowned. "Well, okay, about that part. But why did you leave in the first place? Don't you love us, Maggie?"

Maggie's eyes filled with tears. "Oh, yes, David, I love you. You, and Benny and Chelsey and—" And your father. Oh, David, I love your father so much, but he doesn't love me and I couldn't bear to be there another second because my heart was breaking. "But in order to be a family, a real family, the dad person has to be in love with the mom person and vice versa.

If that isn't the case, then it just won't work. Understand?''

"But my dad *does* love you, we know that, all three of us kids know that, because he talks all gooey about you," David said, then sniffled. "And you talk gooey about him, too, so you love him and I won't believe you if you say you don't. And you two smile weird at each other…you know, like sticky syrup on pancakes or something. Gooey smiles."

"I, um…"

"But then my dad made you cry. Right?" David said, his voice rising. "That is so dumb. He loves you, he made you cry, and you left us. My dad is so stupid, Maggie."

"David, look, there is so much you don't understand," Maggie said. "It's late, you're exhausted and upset, and enough is enough for tonight. You can sleep here, but in the morning I'm going to take you home and—"

"No."

"Yes," she said, gripping his hands. "I need to apologize to Chelsey and Benny, too, for not staying and saying a proper goodbye. As for the rest of this business that's made you so unhappy I— No, not now. Promise me you won't sneak out of here, David. Promise me."

"Okay," he said, sighing. "It's really cold outside."

"Yes, it is. Now, come on," she said, getting to her feet. "I'll tuck you into my bed and I'll sleep here on the sofa. I'm going to call your dad after you're in bed and tell him you're spending the night, and that we'll be over there in the morning."

"I'll go home, but I won't speak to my dad. Not ever again."

"Fine. Finish your hot chocolate."

David was asleep within moments of being tucked beneath the warm blankets on Maggie's bed. She placed one hand gently on his cheek, then kissed him on the forehead.

"You're right about one thing, sweetheart," she whispered. "Grown-ups, not just your dad, can be very, very dumb."

Back in the living room, Maggie called Harrison, who picked up halfway through the first ring.

"Maggie?"

"Yes, it's me, Harrison. David is spending the night here. He's sound asleep. We'll be over there in the morning. I need to apologize to Chelsey and Benny for not saying goodbye to them the way that I should have.

"Then we have to make them understand that sometimes things just don't go the way they hoped and that it's no one's fault and—" Maggie stopped speaking as tears spilled onto her cheeks. "Goodbye."

Harrison held on to the receiver until it buzzed in his ear, announcing it had been off the hook too long and the other party had long since hung up. He put it back into place.

"You're wrong, Maggie," he said, his voice thick with emotion. "This *is* someone's fault. Mine."

At nine o'clock the next morning, David, Chelsey and Benny were sitting on the sofa, both Benny and Chelsey having thumbs firmly in their mouths, while David glowered at his knees.

Maggie pulled an easy chair close to the sofa and gestured to Harrison to do the same.

"First of all," Maggie said, "I want to apologize to you all. I know this is a rerun for you, David, but bear with me. I need to apologize for leaving without saying goodbye to you the way I should have, giving you hugs, telling you I'd see you soon and that I love you very much. I'm saying it now and I'm very sorry for leaving the way that I did."

Chelsey pulled her thumb out of her mouth. "But why did you go, Maggie? I thought you liked it here. We all thought you were gonna be our mom, the mom person, so we could be a family and have a baby and—"

"Yes, I know you thought that," Maggie said, hoping, praying she wouldn't cry, "but you were…you were mistaken, Chelsey. I explained it to David last night. The mom person and the dad person have to be in love with each other or it doesn't work. I'm sorry you're disappointed, but you mustn't blame your father. It's not his fault, don't you see?"

Out popped Benny's thumb. "Not his fault. Thumbs taste yucky, Chelsey. Why are we putting them in our mouths? Icky."

"Yeah, they are icky," Chelsey said, staring at her thumb. "I guess I won't do that anymore."

"That's great," Maggie said, getting to her feet. "Now, do we understand each other? We're friends? I'll see you at the library for story hour?" She had to get out of that house, away from Harrison Parker before she dissolved into a weepy mess on the floor. "Everything is hunky-dory? Yes, it is. So, goodbye for now and—"

"Wait a minute," David yelled.

Maggie was so startled she plunked back onto her chair.

"Our dad made you cry," David went on, volume on high. "I know he did. What about that part? What about my dad being the dumbest person in the whole wide world?"

"Good question," Harrison said, pointing one finger in the air. "And it deserves an answer."

"It does?" Maggie said, staring at him with wide-eyes.

"Yes, it does," Harrison said. "However, I'll get back to you on that, David. Chelsey. Benny. I need to discuss it with Maggie first."

"You do?" she said.

"I do," Harrison said. "You kids bundle up and go outside. The sun is shining and it's not as cold as it was yesterday. I need to talk to Maggie privately."

"I don't want go outside," David said, folding his arms over his chest.

"David, move your tush," Harrison said, in a voice that did not welcome a retort.

"Outside," David said, sliding off the sofa. "Come on, Chelsey, Benny. I'll help you with your buttons and zippers and junk. Hurry up."

In record time the three were in their heavy clothes and the front door slammed closed behind them.

"I don't understand why you did that, Harrison," Maggie said, staring into space. "There really isn't anything for us to discuss. I think you were a tad hasty in promising David an answer to why I must have cried."

"Don't forget the part about my being the dumbest person in the whole wide world," Harrison said, then moved onto the sofa directly in front of Maggie, who continued to look at the far wall. "Look at me, Maggie."

"No, I'd rather not at the moment."

"Please?"

Maggie sighed, then met Harrison's gaze. He leaned forward and grasped both of her hands in both of his.

"You were wrong," he said quietly, "when you told the kids that what happened here wasn't my fault, because it was."

"No, Harrison, I explained to them that it's *no one's* fault if the dad person and the— Oh, for heaven's sake… If the man and woman aren't in love with each other. There's no blame to be placed if feelings, emotions don't match and—''

"Match?" Harrison interrupted. "Meaning you believe that my feelings don't match yours? Meaning that you're in love with me, but I'm not in love with you? That's why you left here, isn't it? That's why you cried?"

Maggie attempted to pull her hands free, but Harrison tightened his hold.

"Damn you, Harrison Parker," Maggie said, her eyes filling with tears. "Won't you leave me with even an ounce of my pride? Let go of my hands. I want to go home."

"No," he said, shaking his head. "Not until I've had my say, not until you've listened to me. Please, Maggie, hear me."

She nodded jerkily, then sniffled.

"Maggie, I lacked the courage of a ten-year-old boy. My son went after what he knew was missing from his life. He set out in the cold and the rain to go to you, because he loves you, needs you, wants you to be a part of his world.

"At the moment I was prepared to pour out my heart to you, I fell prey to my own inner fears, my self-doubts regarding my ability to know how to love someone the way you deserved to be loved. I was so terrified, that I...I blew it. I was, indeed, the dumbest person in the whole wide world."

"But—"

"Let me finish, please," Harrison said, his voice

husky. "Well, thanks to David, I've been given a second chance here and, God help me, I'm going to do this right this time."

He drew a deep, shuddering breath.

"Maggie Conrad, I...I... Damn it, I love you with every breath in my body, all that I am. I can't promise you that I'll be the perfect husband. I'm going to make mistakes, but if you love me as much as I love you, we'll work out whatever we stumble over in the future.

"I swear to you that I won't run from problems we might face. We'll meet them head on, together. Ah, Maggie, I don't want to go through the rest of my life without you. I want to marry you, have a baby with you, grow old and creaky with you and... It's taken every ounce of courage I have to say all that to you."

Harrison released his hold on Maggie's hands and got to his feet.

"Please, Maggie, tell me. Do you love me?" he said, not even attempting to hide the tears glistening in his eyes. "Will you marry me, Maggie Conrad, be my wife for better, for worse, until we no longer exist on this earth and beyond? Maggie? Please?"

Tears spilled onto Maggie cheeks as she launched herself up and into Harrison's embrace, causing him to stagger slightly. She flung her arms around his neck, as his encircled her waist.

"Yes," she said. "Oh, yes, Harrison, I love you. I love you so much, and I'll marry you, and create a beautiful baby with you, and we'll love our children to pieces, and we'll talk our problems through when they come, and maybe we'll even get a puppy and—''

Harrison kissed her. He kissed Maggie to seal their commitment to their forever and she responded in total abandonment, pledging her love to Harrison for all time.

A distant noise caused Harrison to raise his head, glance around, then chuckle. David was knocking on the front window with a mitten-covered hand. Three shivering, rosy-cheeked Parker kids were peering in on the scene taking place in the living room, big, happy smiles on their faces. Maggie laughed in loving delight.

"Come on in here, you hoodlums," Harrison yelled at the grinning trio outside the window. "This family has a wedding to plan!"

* * * * *

*There are more secrets to reveal—
don't miss out!
Coming in April 2004 to
Silhouette Books*

*Gideon Faulkner had lived a life in
captivity, kidnapped and brainwashed
years ago by the Coalition. But he had
found a way to sneak into the outside
world, and finally had a chance to find
his real family...and true love.*

THE INSIDER

By

Ingrid Weaver

Family Secrets: *Five extraordinary
siblings. One dangerous past.
Unlimited potential.*

*And now, for a sneak peek,
just turn the page...*

Prologue

The crowbar slipped, striking sparks from the rock and ripping the leather that covered Gideon's knuckles. The door hadn't been opened since the tunnel had been sealed two decades ago. The damp air inside the mountain had corroded the hinges and cemented the bolt in place. The mechanism no longer worked as it was designed to.

Like him. He was as rusty as this forgotten escape hatch. Frozen in place. Self-destructing from within. Unseen, unknown...

"Get a grip," he muttered, his voice rumbling back from the rock that surrounded him. He repositioned the crowbar. "You're not even out yet and already you're losing it."

Iron scraped against steel. Gideon tested the strength of the lock, but there was no give to the metal. He played his flashlight around the edges of the doorframe, searching for a weak spot where the assembly was bolted to the tunnel wall. The crowbar was a primitive tool, but that and a chisel were all he'd been able to acquire undetected. He could have made explosives, but he wouldn't have been able to use them. Although he was too far from the inhabited areas of the compound for the noise of a blast to be heard, the seismic sensors around the perimeter would pick up the shock wave and someone would be sent to investigate the tunnel.

Gideon wasn't sure what he'd do if they found him. Could he take a life in order to preserve his own? How deep did the evil run in his soul?

Then again, only humans had souls.

And Gideon Faulkner wasn't quite human.

He checked that the rip in his glove hadn't reached his skin, then tightened his grip on the crowbar. Why was he doing this? He was safe here. He was valued. His sprawling quarters were furnished with every luxury that struck his fancy. He had so much wealth he'd needed to design a special program to count it. He had everything....

Except the truth.

He shook his head. That was ironic. Why would a man at the top of the FBI's Most Wanted list care about truth?

He turned to look behind him. The path through the mountain was swallowed by darkness, but he'd memorized every turn when he'd studied the schematic. The airlock that separated his quarters from the rest of the compound emerged too close to a public corridor to risk using, so it had taken weeks of painstaking labour to break through his bedroom wall to this tunnel. Once he had, it had been child's play to disable the alarm system—after all, he'd been in his teens when he'd invented it. The system was meant to keep intruders from getting in.

A person would have to be crazy to break out.

Crazy? Gideon's mind was his greatest asset, yet would he know when he crossed the brink into insanity? It wasn't too late to go back to the compound. For more than twenty years it had been his sanctuary, the only home he'd known. Leaving the safety of his quarters, even for one night, could kill him. The vision that he chased could be an illusion. All he had were fragmented memories of a house by the sea. Dreams of a better place...and a different self.

What if there was no truth out there?

Or worse, what if he didn't like what he found?

With a growl like the warning of a trapped animal, Gideon pushed aside his doubts and swung the crowbar at the door. Vibrations shot up his arms and rattled his teeth. He widened his stance, his muscles bunching, and swung again.

A chunk of rock flew back from the edge of the doorframe. Three more broke loose with the next blow. Gideon jammed the end of the crowbar into the gap and threw his full weight against it.

Metal screeched. Rock crumbled. The bolts that held the doorframe to the tunnel wall snapped. Gideon jumped backward as the door crashed to the floor at his feet.

Dust billowed in a choking cloud. He shielded his face with his arms and held his breath until it settled, then cautiously moved forward. When he filled his lungs once more, he tasted something strange. Something different. A fresh, sharp tang like the soap he used, like the wooden shelves in his library when they had been new.

It took him a heartbeat to realize what he breathed.

It was fresh air.

Damn, he'd done it. He was out.

Gideon grabbed his flashlight and propped the door into place behind him. He had six hours left before he'd be missed. That should be enough time to cover the three miles to town and begin the search for the truth behind his memories. According to the topographical maps, cutting across country would be rough in places until he could parallel the highway, but as long as he didn't encounter something unforeseen—

A monster loomed in front of him, so tall it blocked the sky. Gideon lurched back, directing his flashlight beam upward. Limbs swayed in the darkness, trailing fragrant tendrils through the air. A tree. He recognized it from the pictures he'd studied. It was a hemlock, part of the pocket of old-growth forest surrounding the buildings that concealed the compound.

He reached for a branch and ran his gloved fingers along flat needles slick with mist. He moved deeper into its shadow, his boots slipping on hillocks of moss. His nostrils flared as rich, earthy scents swirled around him. He pressed his hand to the trunk.

Through a protective barrier of supple kidskin, he explored the contours of the bark.

It was dangerous to linger. Precious minutes were passing. This was only a hemlock tree, after all. Nothing special.

He closed his eyes, his senses whirling. Nothing special? Damn, it wasn't a photo in a book or an image on a screen, it was a *real tree*. And for the first time in his life he was touching one, smelling one, hearing the branches sigh in the breeze...

Or was it the first time?

Something danced on the fringe of his consciousness. He felt air on his face, but it wasn't laden with the scents of the forest; it was tinged with salt. The breeze became the crash of waves. Sunshine warmed his skin—

The vision winked out as soon as he reached for it. Gideon pushed away from the tree and began his journey.

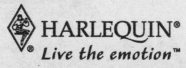

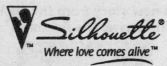

Silhouette ®

Where love comes alive ™

FAMILY SECRETS

Five extraordinary siblings.
One dangerous past.
Unlimited potential.

Collect four (4) original proofs of purchase from the back pages of four (4) Family Secrets titles and receive a specialty themed free gift valued at over $20.00 U.S.!

Just complete the order form and send it, along with four (4) proofs of purchase from four (4) different Family Secrets titles to: Family Secrets, P.O. Box 9047, Buffalo, NY 14269-9047, or P.O. Box 613, Fort Erie, Ontario L2A 5X3.

Name (PLEASE PRINT)

Address   Apt. #

City   State/Prov.   Zip/Postal Code

Please specify which themed gift package(s) you would like to receive:

❏ PASSION DT5N
❏ HOME AND FAMILY DT5P
❏ TENDER AND LIGHTHEARTED DT5Q

❏ Have you enclosed your proofs of purchase?

FAMILY SECRETS

One Proof
Of Purchase
FSPOP10R

Remember—for each package selected, you must send four (4) original proofs of purchase. To receive all three (3) gifts, just send in twelve (12) proofs of purchase, one from each of the 12 Family Secrets titles.

Please allow 4-6 weeks for delivery. Shipping and handling included. Offer good only while quantities last. Offer available in Canada and the U.S. only. Request should be received no later than July 31, 2004. Each proof of purchase should be cut out of the back page ad featuring this offer.

Visit us at www.eHarlequin.com   FSPOP10R